C000048795

THE DAYS (

'As it was in the days of Noah,
so it will be in the days of the coming of
the Son of Man... they knew nothing about
what would happen until the flood came
and took them all away'.

(Matthew's Gospel)

Based on incidents in the
author's life in Perú,
1965-1993

To Juanita

1968

Ten o'clock on the old cathedral clock... The sun streamed in through the high latticed window of the second floor of the old colonial Ministry of Immigration building in the capital. Ernesto could hardly believe it all. He allowed his long finger-nails to run along the edge of the large leather tooled desk as he looked down again at the double sided name plate facing him. Colonel Ernesto Julio Delgado Vargas... A long road for an illegitimate son of Maria Vargas from the village of *Pucayacu* in the Province of *Santa Cruz de la Sierra*. His school friends had called him *gringo*, because of his blue eyes, so unusual in a Latin American. He remembered his grandmother asking him repeatedly if he could see properly?

"Only blind mules and dogs have blue eyes", she affirmed.

Ernesto, *El Gringo*, did not smile when he remembered his father must have been the visiting Irish priest who had possessed his mother, as a girl of fifteen, in his yearly visit to the *Fiesta de la Virgen de Pucayacu*. That was the last time that a priest ever visited the village.

That mud-brick chapel in the small plaza gradually succumbed to indifference, an earthquake and the annual torrential rains that lashed its structure. It was as if the elements were trying to wash away the stain of that act and many other such acts committed during the week of the drunken fiesta activities.

Yes, the stain of blood was never far away in Latin America:

There were the stains of blood from the sweating backs of those who had built the churches under the scourging of the Jesuits' whips; blood from the bull with the condor on its back; blood from the oxen with open sores as they brought the chapel bell across the Andes, five hundred kilometres from the port of *Paita* in the north, from the ship and the foundry in *San Lucar de Barameda* in Spain; blood from the diseased who squatted to relieve themselves by its walls and buttresses; blood from the dead Christ on the plaster cross; blood from the bull fighting in the plaza on "Saints Day"; blood from the child trampled by the horse of the *Patrón* in his mad gallop through the square... It seemed to Ernesto, as a boy, that the rain would never wash the stain of blood away.

Yes, blood marked life, and death in Latin America.

There had been more blood last week too. *"The People's Revolution"* had been quick, but not unexpected. Years of neglect and oppression of the rural and marginalised population of the country had gradually swelled into a festering boil that could easily be lanced by some opportunists. And those that were well placed to grasp the opportunity for their own ends were the military.

The oligarchy, landowners and those who owned the mines were too preoccupied with exporting their wealth and interests in investment and pleasure abroad to realise, perhaps, what was going on around them. Ernesto remembered that their *patrón* Don Diego Trellis Ocampo used to boast how magnanimous he was in giving his *peones* (farm-workers) a set of new clothes, a sack of rice, and as much *trago* (cane alcohol), that they produced on the hacienda, as they wanted, all as their yearly wage. He remembered, too, how his mother's hands were always covered in pustules from the caustic soda and hard soap as she scrubbed daily in cold river water for the family in the *Casa Grande* (Big-house). But Trellis was long gone. He had got wind of the situation and was probably relaxing somewhere in Switzerland, his wife and family in one or another of their homes in the south of France.

The government and the politicians, with their usual self-interest at heart, had either meekly submitted to the coup, protesting that they had always been in favour of "the people", or had sought refuge in various "friendly" embassies in the Capital, claiming that this act was an "outrage" and that the UN or the USA should "step in" and "solve" this "problem".

At dawn on the ninth of October, the tanks had rumbled into the main square of the Capital, in front of the palace; the president and his family had been rudely awakened from their beds and, had been dressed in their nightclothes and borrowed ponchos, to be driven down back streets to the airport and put on an Air-Force DC4 for Venezuela .

There had been a problem, for the Ecuadorian and Colombian governments had refused re-fuelling and rights of passage over their sovereign airspace, so the plane was redirected via Manaus in Brazil, then out over the Atlantic and back inland over Guyana!

The nation's radio and TV stations had been seized and began to emit the prepared messages by General Francisco "*Pancho*" Fernández Alzamora advising the nation of the coup, and that the public in general need not fear a thing, that the days of the *gamonales* were over. They were to be "free at last"! This would be repeated sporadically throughout the days and weeks to follow along with stirring military music and popular songs by local folk-groups and singers from the regions to the music of the *cumbia, salsa, huanyos*", etc., etc.

Provision had been made to "encourage the local communist parties, not that they needed it, to daub slogans on walls and public buildings such as "*Viva la Revolución*"; "*Libertad*"; "*El gamonal no comerá de tu pobreza*" (The landowners will not feast off your poverty); "*PCN*" (The National Communist;Party) "*El pueblo unido jamás será vencido*" (The masses will never be overcome); the odd hammer and sickle sign and outlines of Ché Guevara.

It was true that there were several Marxist-Leninist generals and Communist Party leaders in the Armed Forces, but most were cynical opportunists and saw the Revolution as a way to ensure the permanence of the Armed Forces as ultimate authority, a "managed" nation away from the hands of the twelve or so families whose control over land and the economy had existed since colonial times.

Among the few there was a genuine desire for a socialist transformation where all would be equal and whose rights would be guaranteed. However it would be a sad day, they said, if the country were to fall into the hands of the *masa anónima ignorante* (the amorphous ignorant people). "*Orden, método y disciplina*" (Order, method and discipline) was the motto and the way forward!

But of course, there was still the bloodshed.

Ernesto remembered the old phrase, "*Entre dicho y hecho hay mucho trecho*" (there is a big gulf between what is said and what is done)! He had heard, only yesterday, that in his own village of Pucayacu, the villagers and the *peones* on the nearby *Hacienda Santa Mónica* had ransacked the place.

The local police had opened fire on the looters without warning, and some thirty people had been killed or wounded. All that remained of the building and its contents were strips of wallpaper hanging from the walls and a large pile of newspapers and magazines that the owners received weekly from Europe and the USA. They were deemed useless, as most people were illiterate, and the newspapers were in a foreign language. The bone china crockery was also lying smashed, as it was considered too delicate for daily use in homes that used tin cups and plates. The doors, the roof, the tiles, the windows, even the parquet floors were gone. Timber was useful for cooking fires.

This story was repeated throughout the countryside, while in the city, the majority of the population stayed indoors, only venturing out to see if there were any products available in the market place stalls and small shops.

There had been looting also in the city. On his way into work in his polarized windowed car, followed in convoy by an army *Datsun* pickup, with two men with sub-machine guns on the back, he had see one tall man staggering along balancing a sofa on his head and clutching a TV set in his arms, a little girl behind him trailing a box full of shoes and dresses. Nobody was stopping them.

Ernesto had heard on the radio that the large oil refinery run by Shell Petroleum up north and the oil wells further down in the jungle had been secured and now were to be nationalised and called Petro *Nacional* or *PENA* for short. He wondered how production could be maintained while, although most of the operatives were nationals, the technicians and engineers were from the USA or Venezuela.

"Not my problem", he murmured to himself as he sat in the office and reached for a cigar from the box on the table.

The lucrative fishing industry and its fish-canning plants would also be nationalised and foreign boats would have to land their quotas in the country itself if they wished to fish in the new 200 mile limit that the Revolution had ordained. "Fish for one, fish for all" was the slogan.

Yes, he, Ernesto, had come a long way from that mud hut and rudimentary primary school in the village. He remembered vividly the wrote learning method of reading and writing: "*A with A, spells A; B with B, spells B; C with C spells C...* " and the teacher whacked the board with a cane stick as all shouted in unison, the same thing, time after time, day after day. Well, not really "day", for around 10am the teacher would lead them out to do weeding and watering in his vegetable garden or banana patch and they would be back home again for twelve.

He had been fortunate that a couple of nuns came as teachers whenhe was a little older and they taught writing on slate boards. They also took prayers and woe betide any boy who did not learn the "Hail Mary" or proved disobedient or recalcitrant, for they would be made to kneel on maize grains and say the Lord's Prayer twenty times in punishment.

It seemed to Ernesto that his knees still ached in the damp days in the Capital.

But then, the nuns had given him an opportunity to go to college in the nearby town. There they had a cadet corps and Ernesto enjoyed the discipline and direction of that time, so when he was sixteen he was able to join the army officer school. in the outskirts of the Capital.

That was not all joy and gladness. The first few months of training were basic cruelty and sadism. He was not physically tough enough to qualify for the parachute division or the *Sinchis*, the hard core commando units. But he still had to do degrading things like eat dog meat, bite the heads off rats, smear comrades with faeces, run until he dropped, etc. But he also was able to participate in learning English and Russian and found himself to be peculiarly adept at languages. Hence his being in the post now in the Ministry of Immigration.

••••••••••

The cathedral clock struck the quarter, sending the pigeons in the plaza off in fright, and Ernesto tapped the brass bell on his desk in echo to the chime.

One half of the oak panelled door swung open and a man marched in. He was in many ways in distinct contrast to Ernesto, *El Gringo*. Whereas Ernesto was cool and calculating by nature, this man seemed cheerfully whimsical.

While *El Gringo* had been brought up in the provinces, this man had been brought up in the one of the poorest slum areas of the Capital. Whereas *El Gringo* was by nature conservative and somewhat aloof, this man was the epitome of an urban "*cholo*" culture.

Colonel Ernesto was immaculate, regulation haircut, uniform pressed, shoes gleaming and mirror-like, epaulettes sparkling, shirt and tie ironed crisply, whereas Lieutenant Alberto Sánchez Córdoba had long, lank hair, a greasy local-woven head-band, open-neck black shirt with insignia and the now famous wide leather belt with the brass triangular buckle, the symbol of the Three *Martyrs of Taragona*.

In the seventeenth century, these three men of Taragona had tried to prevent sending twenty thousand Indians to certain death in the gold mines owned by the *encomenderos* (landowners). As a result, the three had been captured and tied together in a human triangle, head to toe, and left to die and desiccate on a glacier on the *Cordillera Blanca* at seventeen thousand feet above sea level.

"Remember Taragona" had been one of the slogans of the Revolution.

It would have been pointless to explain to Alberto that the three were actually Spanish conquistadors, not Indians, and not therefore protagonists of a revolution that was supposedly anti-capitalist, anti-Iberian and ostensibly led by an Indian uprising!

El Gringo disliked Lieutenant Alberto for two reasons. One, he considered Alberto dangerous, due to the fact that Alberto was heavily influenced by Maoist thought. Most leaders of the Revolution were endeavouring to steer a middle course, playing Castro and the Kremlin off against the Chinese, while denouncing North American imperialism, the CIA and Western colonialism. They were all, however, open to North American under-cover arms contracts in order to acquire several fighter aircraft, a couple of post-war navy frigates and a couple of hundred Hummer armoured personnel carriers along with twenty Exocet missiles. Not that they envisaged war with their neighbours, but rather in order to bolster National Armed Forces prestige on parades and displays.

The Armed Forces always had to be top of the totem pole, Ernesto reminded himself.

Alberto was also dangerous in *El Gringo*'s eyes, because of his good looks and ways with the ladies, despite his unkempt exterior. He would never take "no" for an answer.

They had both been appointed to the Ministry of Immigration as Director and Sub-director, not because the posts were of prime importance to the Revolution and the Agrarian Reform, nor were they considered to be among the intellectuals and generals who knew what the score was, but they were presentable and diligent and would, as it were, be the "honest face" of the Revolution for those who were seeking entrance into the county for residence, diplomacy or trade.

It cut both ways, for Alberto and *El Gringo* saw it as a step on the ladder to being nominated a "General".

The post of "General" meant houses and land, a pension that would see one in clover for the rest of one's days after fifty; four or five trips a year to "events" internationally; cars and a summer villa on the coast somewhere. Alberto imagined himself following his beloved national soccer team round the world with a bevvy of beauties, while *El Gringo* saw himself married again, on a large farm and vineyard and still having the luxury of it managed and run by those who foolishly believed that *La Reforma* would bring them autonomy and land ownership.

The post in Immigration itself would require no great effort on Ernesto, *El Gringo*'s, part, just to be at his desk at ten 'til twelve; three hours then for siesta, and an hour from three 'til four to sign off any documents, visas and the like.

Alberto, on the other hand, would have to be around from nine, in case there were any "emergencies" and work another hour in the afternoon to "clear things up" and see to the closure of the office. Of course there would be the usual holidays, saints days, famous "victory" days, memorial days and the like, so it would work out on average about twenty days a month.

His car and military escort would whizz Ernesto to his house in the foothills, thirty kilometres outside the Capital, or to his beach-house in the gated community military recreation and sports centre.

There was no dichotomy in *El Gringo*'s thinking between his lifestyle and ethos of the Revolution, daubed on the wall across the square, *"Equality and Opportunity for all!"*

But there was another advantage for Alberto, and *El Gringo* had been right to be wary of him, for in the office there was a large female presence from typists to cashiers!

He was right too in another sense, but completely unaware of it at that moment, that Alberto was a "sleeper" for the KJB and had been so since Ché Guevara had been to Peru and Bolivia.

Alberto had been recruited when he was an out-of-work seventeen year old. There was something almost Teutonic about the KJB spy system in Latin America. Whereas the CIA had "key men" in "key places", the KJB had planted informers at all levels of society, in both urban and rural situations, in social aid organisations, football associations, trade unions, educational institutions, and the like.

Many of them would never be activated, but they were there *por si acaso* (just in case). The Chinese espionage had barely gotten off the ground, but their methodology in turn was to flood the market with cheap comic strips showing the wonders of chairman Mao and of China as a place to visit, along with stories of "derring do" of Ninjas, swordsmen and the like, and simplified technical information on the latest Chinese engineering prowess.

Alberto had been brought up in one of the capital's roughest slums, called *La Jungla* and had gone to school almost as a protest against society at large! His mother had been the only true and stable influence on his early life. He had never known his father. His mother used to tell him that he had gone off to the jungle to work in the gold mines and would be back soon. But he never had appeared.

His mother had cajoled Alberto, pummelled him, wheedled and shouted at him by turns throughout his school and college days. He really preferred to lounge around at the street corner, play football in a dusty vacant lot with his mates, an area that served as a latrine at night and a playground by day. One of the neighbours kept a pig there which acted as a lavatory attendant and sewage disposal system for the street. But if he hated school with a perfect hatred, he loved his mother and protected her with an equal passion and ferocity.

Alberto had returned one evening after football to find his mother on the floor of their one roomed home in a narrow alleyway, making strange groaning noises. Her round flat face was streaming with perspiration even though the night was chilly at that time of year. Her bananas, avocados, prickly pears lay scattered around her from the wicker basket that must have been perched on her head as she returned from street selling. Her fleshy hands were squeezed tight like two large balls and her ample bosom heaved irregularly. Her eyes stared vacantly at the bamboo ceiling with its spiders' webs.

Alberto was terrified.

He turned and ran down three blocks to the clinic to seek the *sanitario* (first-aid man). He was drunk, as usual, playing poker with two acquaintances, and at first outrightly refused to come, saying it was two dollars, cash, for a house call after six. That was more than Alberto ever earned at car-washing on the street-crossing in a day. Alberto begged, threatened, but the first-aid man looked across the greasy table and with bleary eyes, shrugged his shoulders and muttered,

"What can one do? It must have been her *suerte* (destiny/luck)…We all have to die sometime, I'm very sorry".

Alberto was about to grab him and smash his face in, when a *Serrano* (a highlander) who had been sitting reading a booklet in the corner, jumped up and stood between them.

He thrust two dollars into the *sanitario*'s shirt pocket. The *sanitario* stood up unsteadily, took down his emergency aid case and shuffled off behind Alberto who began to walk quickly on ahead.

The *Serrano* followed them both, chewing on his *"coca"* wad. It was too late. His mother lay relaxed now on the floor, still staring at the spiders in the roof. She would not need the "tender" administrations of the *sanitario*.

Alberto began to cry and wail and beat his forehead against the paper thin walls of their home. The *sanitario*, after falling on the woman's body in a drunken attempt to ascertain if she still breathed, shoved himself into a kneeling position and with a shaky hand scrawled a note:

"I certify that....

What's her name...?", he asked over his shoulder

"María Córdoba Aspajo", sobbed Alberto

The first-aid man added the name and continued to write:

'Died of a heart-attack at 20.32 on the date below.'

He took from his satchel a rubber stamp with his name and number on it, breathed heavily on the stamp face to dampen it, pressed it on the paper and dated and signed with an unintelligible flourish.

"Five dollars, please".

He addressed the surrounding bystanders who had silently filtered in after hearing the cries of anguish. Again the *Serrano* dug into his ragged woollen trouser pocket and fished out a greasy five dollar bill.

The first-aid man then promptly fell asleep in the corner. Only the Serrano and the neighbours seemed to know what to do next.

They lifted his mother on to the table, covered her with a sheet from the bed in the corner. The *Serrano* then went out and bought a small keg of rum, several bottles of the local beer and six candles. He lit one candle and dribbled the wax on the table to steady it then proceeded to place two others at María's head and three at her feet.

He then scattered some ashes from the cooking stove over the threshold of the door.

"We don't want her spirit to come back in and take possession of her body and turn her into a zombie", he reminded them. "The cross will keep the devil at bay", marking the door with a charcoal ember from the stove.

They sat round María's body all night as the candles guttered and cast grotesque shadows on the walls as the neighbours came and went.

Around six in the morning, as it was getting light, a thud at the door startled some. It was the undertaker with a coffin of hastily tacked together timbers and daubed with a white powdered lime covering.

"What would your mother wish to take with her?" The *Serrano* asked Alberto.

"I don't know…" gulped Alberto.

"Well, let me suggest that she takes some toasted maize and a can of *Fanta* as the journey is a long one over the moors to the *River of Jordan*, or the *River of Blood* as some call it, and maybe a shawl and shoes as there are lots of thorns and sharp stones that would tear her soul on the pathway to Heaven".

As they heaved the coffin onto the back of an old *Chevvy* pickup, the *Serrano* asked Alberto if they had had a dog?

"Yes, we used to have a mongrel called *Layqa*, but it was run over by a *Volvo* truck".

"What colour was it?" asked the *Serrano*

"Well, it was sort of browny-black, why?"

"Well it'll be there at the *River of Jordon* to drag your mother's soul over to the *Gate of Heaven*, but if it had been a whitish dog it would never have gone in the river as it is always dirty. Didn't you know these things?" The *Serrano* looked long and hard at Alberto. He felt sorry for him. He had a lot to learn.

The cemetery was not too far away. Because of the increasing population of the city and the *invasiones* of farmland and desert on the outskirts, the Council had designated a rough piece of hillside as a burial ground, while designating a better piece of flat land for the construction of rows of *nichos* ten high, for the more affluent of the population.

The poor could just dig a hole and bury their dead on the hill. The ground had been consecrated by the Roman Catholic Church so only Catholics could be buried there. Jews, Protestants and other faiths would have to make other arrangements. An impressive concrete cross with a serpent-like angel coiled around it dominated the scene. Alberto thought it really creepy.

They staggered up the slope with the heavy coffin (Maria had been all of one hundred and ten kilos) and found an open grave awaiting them. Two alcoholic diggers were there clutching their knees and sitting on a mound of earth, their picks and shovels strewn about like the remains of an ancient battlefield. There was no priest or official to officiate, so the coffin was lowered down on two ropes by the gravediggers, the *Serrano* and Alberto.

The *Serrano* crossed himself and kissed his thumb. Alberto was too moved to do anything except sigh. The grave diggers started shovelling and in a trice the shallow grave was filled, the extra earth piled up in a sausage shape on the top.

Then the soil was tamped down with a *Takana rumi*, a big stone blessed by the priest, that the gravediggers raised over their heads and let it crash down, time and again, on the mound.

"We don't want her rising on all-saints day!", they joked.

"Why don't you put some thorns over the grave?", suggested the *Serrano*. "Then, if she does rise as a *condenada* (a ghoul), she'll feel the thorns pricking her and think it is God's fire-rain on the last-judgement day!".

"Naw", said one of the other grave-diggers, "we only do that for the *evangelistas* (protestant-evangelicals). They get rejected every time by Saint Peter and come back to earth as wandering souls and incorporate themselves in other people's bodies or in the dead".

One of them took another swig of *trago* (cane-alcohol) from an old wine bottle, then he placed a simple wooden cross at the head of the grave, made of two ice-lolly sticks.

"Let's go", said the *Serrano*,

"Let's go then", said Alberto and they set off down the hill.

"Born just to die", said the gravedigger to his friend as they began to dig a tiny grave for a still-born child.

"That's so", replied the other, "but why is it that *La mala hierba nunca muere*' (Wickedness never ceases)"!

When they reached the road again, the *Serrano* turned to Alberto and said,

"Why don't you come and stay at my place? Now that your mum's gone, how will you pay the rent and what is there for you?" Alberto thought for a minute, shrugged his shoulders and said, "Why not?"

The *Serrano* was as good as his word, but over his late teenage years he plied Alberto with books by Marx, Lenin and Trotsky, as well as introducing him to the *PCN (Partido Comunista Nacional)*. His introduction was not just theoretical. They participated in encouraging strike actions, worked in soup kitchens in the shanty towns, and at night daubed slogans on bridges, tunnel entrances, and municipal buildings.

Alberto didn't much like the *Serrano*'s cooking, potatoes, *cancha* (toasted maize) or *mote* (boiled maize) and *cuy* (guinea-pig) that ran about the kitchen floor. He had been used to rice and beans and boiled green plantains with his mum. But food was food for a growing man!

When Alberto was nineteen the *Serrano* encouraged him to enter the army, ostensibly abandon his communist past and become a "right-wing devotee", while at the same time begin his subversive activities as an informant and sleeper for the *PCN* and its Russian affiliation.

········

Ten years later Alberto would find himself in the office alongside *El Gringo* in the Immigration Ministry

But the *Serrano* would still be there, watching and waiting.

Ernesto returned from lunch in a nearby restaurant around two-thirty. He felt pleasantly at one with the world and could still taste his *ceviche mixto* (a delicacy of raw fish and sea foods, including octopus, marinated in lemon juice and chilli) on his lips.

There on his desk was the day-book of *"Non-immigrant Resident Visa Requests"*. Normally it would have been the case to sign this off; the process of issuing or re-issuing these visas would be passed to the lower echelons of the Immigration Department to process them and within a week or so issue them to the applicants.

However Ernesto was curious so see who was around in his country and what was their purpose of wishing to be here. He could see no obvious reason why anyone would wish to live or work here rather than in more opulent or progressive countries round the world, especially at this time of social, political and economic destabilisation.

It would be interesting to spot trends and he couldn't just stare out the window all afternoon as his predecessor had done! After all, it was now *"Positions for the Prepared"*, or something like that, on the new party posters.

So *El Gringo* began to look through the last few weeks of entries and make a rough table of entrants' professions.

Engineers   286   (most of them to do with the oil/mining industries)
Technicians   111
Students   39
Administrators and Embassy staff 63
Sales and Business officials   41
Missionaries   29
Priests   6
Teachers   12
Others   40

While Ernesto could see that the figures for Engineers and Technicians were in accord with the party's principles of getting aid from Cuba, Japan and Russia for the nationalised mining and petroleum industries, that was not the figure that caught his eye.

It was that number, the number 29!

He had been born on the 29th. of July; the feast day of the *Little Virgen of Carmen*; it had been in the 29th. year of his life that his wife Mona had left him, saying she didn't love him any more, and went off to live in Venezuela. Then on the 29th of May the following year his young son had been killed on a school outing in a train accident near Cuzco, caused by a landslide, where the 96 people fell 1,500 feet to the raging Urubamba river below.

Twenty-nine, twenty-nine ….And here were twenty-nine missionaries, *gringo* missionaries, and it had been a missionary priest his mother told him that… blue eyes… blind eyes….

And his son might have been in the army cadets by now….!

What were these 29 folks doing here now? Were they too part of that curse that his grandmother had "read" in the *coca* leaves and the entrails of a guinea-pig… ?

What was it she intoned, all those years ago?

'Twenty-nine, Day of the feast,
Twenty-nine, Day of rest,
Twenty-nine, Day of sorrow,
Not once or twice but thrice,
Tomorrow'

Foolish to listen to old wives tales, but his wife, Mona, was gone, and his son, Eduardo, gone and was there a third tragedy yet to come… ?

Would it be somehow connected with these missionaries?

The figure twenty-nine seemed to grow and swell on his paper like some malignant tumour.

He hit the bell on the table with such ferocity that he surprised himself! Alberto, who had been in the outer office chatting up one of the new secretaries in the typing pool, lumbered in.

"Make me a copy of the missionaries listed in this latest list in the book", Ernesto ordered.

Alberto took the book back through to the heavy, clunky photo-copying machine in the corner of the outer office and asked a secretary to make a copy of the missionary entries for the year.

"Ah, Lieutenant, I am so sorry, the machine is "in a state of rest" at the moment, as all the ink was used up in distributing the twenty-page political statement to all the staff about the Revolution. We have ordered new ink but the request has to go through the new finance department… "

She shrugged her shoulders,

"Perhaps it will be available at the beginning of next month. I am sorry, my *Jefe*".

"Well, type them out by hand then", growled Alberto.

Alberto's good humour appeared to have left him. Perhaps it was because it was nearly break time!

He walked back into Ernesto's office as the secretary began the laborious task of copying on the typewriter the names, dates of birth, nationality, local address and occupation of the twenty-nine names in the list.

Ernesto explained to Alberto that he was not signing off these new requests for residential visas or their renewals at the moment. He was to leave the supplicants in limbo. Probably they would never question the delay as there had never been a fixed time scale for approval or disapproval of visas, and the people would not be able to do much about their situations while their passports remained in a drawer somewhere in the offices!

There had been and continued to be a lot of pressure from communist, capitalist and fascists states on his country, so also it would be interesting to see if there was any evidence of that in these twenty-nine names.

Time passed slowly in the office...

At last, the door opened again and Alberto brought in a couple of sheets of paper with the names and details. Ernesto took the list, smoothed it out on the desk and turned to the hovering Alberto.

"Listen, *cholo*, I want you to check out all these people, the twenty-nine that have applied for new or continuing residence. Find out if they are involved in anything suspicious, where they work and what they do and if they are dodgy then we'll have them out!"

A kaleidoscope of pictures flitted through Ernesto's mind as he scrutinised the list:

5037335 Charles Paul Watkins 54, USA Mission Director (renewal)
5037336 Doris Watkins 55, USA Wife (renewal)
6069123 Marvin Klunk, 28, USA, Missionary farmer
6069124 Marylou Klunk 28, USA Wife
6069125 Violet Klunk 9, USA Child
6069126 Daisy Klunk 7, USA Child
6069127 Mervin Junior Klunk 3, USA Child
6069128 Sheniah Jane Klunk 1, USA Child
5769119 Donald Macdonald 40, Scotland, Missionary (renewal)
5769120 Shona Macdonald 39, Scotland, Wife (renewal)
5046861 Leslie Wilson Penner 42, Canada, Missionary (renewal)
5046862 Jodie Penner 40 Canada, Wife (renewal)
5046863 John Edward Penner 17, Canada , Child (renewal)
5046864 Brenda Penner 15, Canada, Child (renewal)
5943622 Harold Spink 25, New Zealand, Missionary

5943623   Martha Spink 26, New Zealand, Wife
5969131   Mary Jane Brown 26, GB, Missionary nurse (renewal)
5042124   Jessica Short 55, GB, Missionary nurse-midwife (renwal)
6069149   Hans De Groot 25, Holland, Missionary
6069150   Nelly De Groot 26 Holland, Missionary
5038213   Daniel Jenkins 60, GB, Medical Missionary (renewal)
5038214   Megan Jenkins 62, Great Britain, Wife (renewal)
5049825   David Greig Possilthwaite 48, GB, Missionary (renewal)
5049826   Margaret Jemima Possilthwaite 44, GB, Wife (renewal)
6069138   Joseph William Richards 29, Jamaica, Missionary
6057071   Mark Mackay Burns 29, Australia, Missionary
6057072   Sheila Burns 29, Australia, Wife
6057073   Robert Howard Burns 5, Australia, Child
6057074   Deborah Maureen Burns 3, Australia, Child

Ernesto saw again the graveside on All-saints day where his mother lay, the meeting of the local dignitaries who had the *carga* for the fiesta that day, florid and uncomfortable in their ill-fitting suits, staggering and sweating under the huge image of *Saint Peter of the Cock-Crow* as they went from "station" to "station" followed by the *prophet*, a scrawny man with long hair, beating his breast with a knobbly club and doing the same at nightfall to his wife in the dark of their home.

Alberto protested…

"Do you mean I'm supposed to search for and question all twenty-nine? Colonel, that would take a life-time! What's going to happen to the Ministry if I'm away for months on end?"

He was also thinking about his forthcoming annual holiday and that Flor, the new typist, had agreed to come with him to the coast for the holiday month.

"Ah, well, you are right", conceded Ernesto. He was beginning to feel a little foolish about his superstitions and personal problems, but he couldn't lose face now.

"However, you could check on most of them in a month and we could fix that up by saying you were on paid sick leave from the start of the month and then report back to me on, say, July 29th., Just get some good evidence for me for keeping or refusing them!"

El Gringo smiled to himself. He could make Alberto responsible for the decision that way and cover himself.

"We can just go slow on business here for the month, and I'll deal with any important visas that need to be granted for engineers and technicians and the like for our "mother country".

Alberto grinned, but then added,

"What about expenses for this business? I'll have to stay and travel all over the place!".

"Okay," replied *El Gringo*, "here's what we'll do. We'll make up an '*Impuesto-ayuda a los pobres, mes de julio, $30*' for all visas, (A tax to help the poor in the month of July for 30 dollars). We'll print it "in-house" and get the treasurer to issue the notice with their request document! Then we'll get the treasurer to collect it separately, give him 10% and we'll use the rest for your trip, less my 15% for the idea!"

"Then, if anyone questions it, we'll say that it came from the Ministry of Economy and Finances and the money went back over there. We'll get the missionaries and others to pay for it themselves!"

It was Alberto's turn to laugh.

Ernesto folded the list carefully and stuffed it into his jacket pocket. Time enough to look at it at home later.

Three-thirty… Time to leave the office.

He locked the desk drawer, and rising, took one more glance across the square,

The shadow of the cathedral tower bisected the square into two uneven portions of strong sunlight in which one was characterised by a small scruffy black tank and the other a group of school children gawping at the cathedral's ornately carved walls.

He closed the shutters and made his way out down the marble staircase, returning the guards' salute at the door, and out into the warm summer sunshine.

"Stupid man!", Ernesto shouted at the beggar at the corner of the main office door. "Why don't you look where you're sitting! You are a disgrace to the Revolution! Off you go and find some work, or you'll be charged and locked up!"

The words came out involuntarily, as he had been miles away thinking about where he was going for the evening: the tennis club by the beach? the horse racing? a soccer match? or perhaps a quiet evening with a couple of beers and a home video?

The beggar's can rolled into the road and was crushed by a passing bus. Ernesto continued on his way round to the underground car-park where his transport awaited him.. He decided on the beers and the video and the scrutiny of this list at home. He instructed his driver and accompanying guard vehicle to take him across the city to his home, up in the green foothills, by the river, where the military HQ was.

"The military is in command… There have been no incidents… Please remain calm and carry on as normal… Long live the Revolution…. *El pueblo unido jamás será vencido* (People who are united will never be defeated)!".

Radio and television were blaring this propaganda out all over the city as he left, but 'the blood' also went on crying out as it had done for the last five hundred years or more.

Ernesto set off in the large BMW saloon and its attendant pick-up through one of the poorer districts to the HQ in the north of the city. There obviously had been some sort of resistance shown to the coup in this sector.

Every now and again there there were odd roadside shapes, covered with newspapers, turning slowly crimson and black in the evening sun.

Surely that one was the remains of a child…?

How different this looked from that "little angel", his young brother, in his little coffin, lime-washed and surrounded by carnations and local lilies, the candles and the village violinist, drunk as usual; his friends playing with frogs, tying cotton wool to their backs and setting them alight to see them jump and squirm. There was laughter and the warmth of home in that death. Here, the blood screamed only, 'Sorrow and Injustice'.

His housekeeper had prepared coffee and a large pile of *churros,* and, with two bottles of *chelas*, the local beer, from his fridge, Ernesto settled down in his favourite chair, tuned the radio on to '*Radio 710 : Melodies For The Moment*' and smoothed out the paper with the list before him. He began to realise that the list didn't tell him very much. He could see that several people had been there for some time by the number of their *carnet* and that they were now up for a two-year renewal.

The military had decided to reduce residency from five years to two, firstly to ensure that that they could terminate "difficult" people's stay more easily, but also they could make more money in the more frequent renewal fee!

The others on the list were all in the process of application. They would have already filled in a preliminary application form in their embassies or consulate in their own country, then on arrival they would have begun the process for an '*Immigrant non-resident*' visa.

That process would have included a visit to the local Police station to fill in a form for verification of residence somewhere in the district. That, of course, would be in triplicate and would cost around twenty dollars per person in the family. The police were then supposed to visit the home to check on the veracity of domicile - though usually, for a little "extra", that process was dispensed with - before the applicants could then return a week or so later and receive two copies with all the necessary stamps on them.

At the same time, a medical examination would be required in a relatively inaccessible building in the centre of the Capital, with hours of service limited to a couple of hours in the morning and a couple in the afternoon. This was supposedly to check for TB, AIDS and Hepatitis B.

Ernesto had been told by his friend Dr.Tulio Labrini, who worked part-time in that clinic, when not in his private practice, that all it was nowadays was really a money-making front for the hospital behind it.

"The X-RAY machine is broken and not actually plugged in, but we go through the motions, then we take off a quantity of blood from each person, supposedly for tests, but we use the blood for the blood services in the hospital, for as you know, *compadre*, all those who come nowadays are healthy and we never have enough blood for emergency cases. We charge $50 dollars per person for the tests and we limit ourselves to twenty people per day so we could make about twenty thousand dollars a month out of it! It's not bad and the immigrant people are happy 'cos they like our "certificate" as it's got a picture of *Macchu Picchu* as its background!"

Then, Ernesto remembered that, of course, immigrants would normally need an "agent" to present the documents, passport and certificates to his offices. These "agents" were usually to be found hanging round the entrance, sometimes squatting beside a box with a typewriter, ready to fill in the appropriate form and letter of application.

Forms and official writing paper for official letters were available at the local newsagents, but for a fee the agent would take care of all the *pormenores* (little details) and folks could go home until the agent called to advise of the time for presenting themselves for photographs and fingerprints, if they were first-time applicants.

Ernesto had seen the immigrants, as he entered the foyer of the ministry, lined up on uncomfortable oak benches with the agents hovering around like bats and shepherding them to one window after another.

The windows were numbered 1 through 5 to present the papers and documents, and then to receive the three copies of the deposit slip. Windows 6-10 were to pay the necessary fees. So, window 6 to get the form to do so; window 7 to pay in dollars; window 8 to receive the money again in local currency, then at window 9 to deposit that money in local currency and finally, at window 10 to receive the final stamps and two copies of the acknowledgement of payment and receipts! Some thirty-four stamps in all!

He had caught the sounds of folks complaining about all sorts of things.
"… the lady in window 8 is always putting nail polish on her nails";
"… the man in number 6 is always going off somewhere else!";
"… the ink on the stamp from number 10 is always wet and messy!"

That would be usually a morning's work for immigrants and it was only open to the public in the mornings. Unless they had an agent on the inside of the system, as did the embassies and some major businesses, they would have to return for another wooden bench and wait for 'finger-prints and camera'.

The finger-print section was in a back room down a narrow windowless corridor on the second floor. There was always jostling between those going in and those coming out and a singular lack of cotton waste to cleanse blackened finger tips. Worst of all was that babies tended to rub their faces with their tiny blackened finger tips and some looked like dervishes on the way out!

In the photographic section, it was a struggle for a parent to hold up a plump baby of ten or eleven months of age, at arms length, sideways on, to have its photo taken, both front and side elevation! Not only were babies reduced to tears by the process but parents as well.

Ernesto could see no way of resolving these issues. These steps in the process had to be done. People's jobs were at stake!

Turning again to the list, he began to think that the best way of starting the process would be for him to go and talk with this mission director man, C. P. Watkins. He would probably know all the others, and where they might be found. His address would be here in the capital somewhere and a visit could be something he could accomplish in a morning and then select the others for Alberto to track down.

He made a mental note to get a secretary to make an appointment with this C. P. Watkins fellow and localise the address.

•••••••••••••••••••

ERNESTO'S FIRST ENCOUNTER

"Holy Moly!" , said C.P. to himself as he put the phone down.

C. P. Watkins, director of the *South American Andean Mission, (SAAM)*, formerly known as the *South American Indian Mission (SAIM)*, looked at the scribbled note he had just written down:

'Colonel Ernesto Delgado, Min. de Inmigración, 10.30 am.'

"What's that all about?", he mused.

"Never had any bother with these people before and normally our agency people take care of all that hog-wash".

"Doris", he yelled down the stairs, "we've got trouble!"

Doris, a dyed blonde haired lady climbed the stairs slowly. She wasn't as young as she used to be and twenty years in the altitude in the southern highlands of the country, four grown-up kids and a 24/7 husband hadn't helped much.

"What is it, honey?"

"We've got this guy coming from the Dept. of Immigration in an hour's time. His secy. says he wants to know about the mission 'n stuff".

"Well, dear, I guess you're the man, you've seen it, done it, got the T-shirt and we ain't had no hassle in the last twenty years, nor any of our folks who went before, except for Hank Williams who ran that guy down with his pickup, way back in the fall of '52".We've just been preachers of the Holy Gospel, no more no less, not like some of these new folks, what you call 'Neo-Evangelicals' and 'Neo-Pentecostals, nor the 'Liberals' that used to be around in the forties. How many churches have we got now, it's more than a hundred and fifty, ain't it, all over the country?"

C. P. leaned back in his big leather chair and looked at the picture of the founder of the mission on the wall before him.

"That's true, changed days since Josiah Partridge arrived here in 1886. Who would have thought that he would have survived his time, his three years in prison for preaching the Word; having his house burned down by the priests; the typhoid epidemic that killed half the town he was in and. all that persecution because the Constitution of the Republic didn't allow anything but Roman Catholicism to be practised here."

Doris poked him in the ribs. "And don't you forget he had a wife, Helen, who never figures much in the photos or the story. It was her ministry as a nurse-midwife that opened the hearts and door of the many! Better tidy up your desk and put some of these books and papers away! I'll get some coffee and cookies ready."

C.P. began to gather up his manuscript papers. He was in the process of writing a book on the contributions to theology and mission studies by up-coming Latin-American Christian writers. He found it hard to admit that some of these "young-guns" were beginning to know more about sociology, politics, cosmology, theology and even Latin-American Church History than he did!

"Most of them are 'commies', though," he consoled himself!

He was to be surprised that, on the dot of 10.30 am., the front door bell of the outer patio rang.

"Mmmm… unusual, if that's him. Never known a Latin-American to be on time for anything!"

C.P. peered cautiously out of the window that overlooked the outer patio. Sure enough, it was a military sort of gentleman being received at the door by the boy. "The boy" was actually 40 years of age and had worked for the mission since he was fourteen. C.P. wasn't even sure of his full surname. He knew it was Mateo something Cruz and that he lived in a small room at the back of the first patio.

It was usual to receive Latin-Americans in a room off the outer patio. The rules had been quite strict when C.P. first came, that no Latin Americans were ever allowed into the inner patio, as one could not trust them. That had been relaxed a little, as there were no other resident families in the buildings now and the rooms were only used for those travelling from their homes in their own countries to and from their "*stations*" elsewhere in the country. There were now no mules tethered in the outer patio these days either, that had been the main form of transport before trucks and buses. Someone had commented that once the missionaries got mechanised transport, they lost personal contact with the mainly pedestrian population!

C.P. sat down in the chair in his office, adjusted his tie, and waited for the knock on the door. A sharp tap followed.

"Come in!" said C.P. in Spanish, in a loud voice.

Ernesto entered the room and saw a grey haired spectacled man behind a large desk.

"Good Morning", Ernesto said, and waited for the man to rise and give a customary handshake and a 'Good Morning' in reply.

Nothing happened!

"Sit down, please," said C.P., waving his hand towards a chair near the door.

.Ernesto felt uncomfortable…

This man was surely quite arrogant and wished to distance himself from any informal conversation! The Spanish cultural distance between them signalled that of cool formality. C.P. was unaware of that, nor appreciated the fact that he should have got up, shaken Ernesto's hand and drawn a chair for him up closer.

Ernesto began diffidently...

"Señor Watkins, forgive the molestation. It occurred to me that, as Director of Immigration in the new democratic revolutionary government, I should make myself known personally to you as director of an entity that has been in our country for a number of years and to enquire of you something of your contribution to the life and development of this, our nation. We are planning on limiting the number of so-called missionary visas, for we are not quite aware of the contribution you are making, if any, to our country."

C.P. took a slow intake of breath. This looked serious.

The work was just beginning to take off, and he felt that foreign missionaries were needed to staff the new Bible Institutes and Seminary; the hospitals and clinics; the Bible translation work into the many various tribal languages, and some of the other medical and literacy programmes that were taking place, let alone to preach the Gospel and get the unsaved into the Kingdom of God.

"Well, Colonel, I guess you don't realise the contribution that missionaries have made and are making throughout your country in many different ways. You don't really want to limit the numbers, you should be increasing the numbers! I reckon we could employ around a thousand to get the job done that we need to do!"

Ernesto was somewhat taken aback by this forthright attitude. This was not the kind of diplomatic language he had expected. At that moment the door opened and Doris came in with a teapot, milk and sugar and some home-baked cookies.

Ernesto leapt to his feet, and took the tray from her hand and set it down on the director's desk. He noticed that C.P. had made no effort to rise in the presence of a lady or to help.

"Oh, that's my wife", was C.P.'s only comment.

Ernesto never drank tea, only coffee, but he pretended to look grateful and sipped it suspiciously. The cookies weren't too bad though, but he limited himself to just one.

After a moment or two, Ernesto produced the list and asked C.P. if he knew these others on the list and if he could help identify what it was they actually did and where they might be stationed at the moment. He thought the use of the word "*station*" was a bit odd as there were no functioning passenger railroads in the country at the moment!

C.P. peered over the top of his spectacles and began by saying,

"You have to understand there are a number of different missionary societies and independent missionary works here. Back in 1916 there was a big missions' conference in Panama and the missionary societies decided to divide off the countries and the areas of each country so that there would be no squabbles among themselves and everywhere might be reached with the Gospel."

Ernesto wasn't quite clear what this "gospel" thing was, but he listened attentively.

"So, for example in your country, one group was allocated the Southern Highlands; another group the jungle area. The Pentecostals were given the most inaccessible areas, as the other missions were wary of them, as they were considered extremists and had only been around since 1910 in the States! The Presbyterians from Scotland were given the highland areas as they were reckoned to be like their own rugged and backward countries. The Methodists had already established themselves here in the capital along with the Anglicans with work among the English business population.

But all that is a bit less rigid nowadays as we all work under a *National Evangelical Council* of which I am the General Secretary, so I guess I should know all those who are on the list here.

Let's see…

Well, the Klunk family have just arrived from Big Fork, Montana and hope to work in the area of jungle clearance where you guys are felling everything to make way for cattle ranching. Marvin had his own spread in Montana and was raising pedigree shorthorns and hopes to be able to help farmers down that way.

The Macdonalds are with a group who work among the Quechua Indian communities and have been here for a year or two. I can't say where they are, they move about a bit, kinda independent folks…;

The Penners have been here for fifteen years or more and work up in the north-east somewhere, good solid folks, keep their heads down and have established churches all over that area…"

Ernesto was beginning to see that following any or all of these people wasn't going to be easy at all for Alberto!

"Now the Spinks, I believe he's a former "all-black."

"Excuse me," interrupted Ernesto, "He's a Maori or an African?"

C.P. laughed. "Nope, he played for New Zealand's Rugby Football team! So he's a tough cookie".

Ernesto was none the wiser, but he let it go.

"The Brown girl is a nurse-midwife and she's going up to the hospital clinic in the Highlands near Wakrapata to accompany the Short lady. Actually she ain't at all "short "at six feet!""

C.P.'s swivel chair squeaked in unison with his laugh.

Ernesto carried on scribbling down all this information on his copy.

"Now Hans and Nelly de Groot are the first missionaries here from Holland. They had hoped to go to South Africa but because of the Apartheid conflict, the missionary society refused to let them go. When I was there in Holland for a conference, the black delegates refused to sleep in the same room with me and the conference ended in a semi riot with the TV there! Some of the Latin Americans supported the black South Africans and they were accused of being Marxists! Weird affair…

"If you want to speak to someone who knows about the Highland work you ought to go and visit the Jenkins. They have been here for nearly forty years and speak Quechua as well as Spanish. They know what's going on and they told me they think there is another Revolution about to happen that is more radical than yours! They also know quite a bit about the cocaine business, not that they are personally involved, of course!

"Can't tell you anything about the Possilthwaites, they have recently arrived and wanted to start an orphanage for street children up the coast somewhere."

"I see there is a Jamaican on the list", said Ernesto.

"Yes, that's so. One of the missions on the coast do quite a bit of work among the *sambitos*, the black folks, in the big sugar plantations and they thought a black person might get on better with them. But I don't know how your government will affect things up there as you are nationalising the sugar production. Tricky business, I imagine…"

Ernesto said nothing. He knew that the country was woefully short of national technicians and business people. The huge sugar plantation at San Jacinto was at a standstill since the revolution, due to the departure of the processing engineers and now the sugar-cane was shrivelling in the fields as the irrigation system was not functioning either.

"So what about this last family on the list, from Australia?"

C.P. stroked his chin.

"I don't know anything about them. They are independents. I think he is a pilot and has some ideas about starting a jungle air service for missionaries and communities along the Amazon and its tributaries. They are going to settle in at Topacocha down there on the Santiago river that feeds into the Amazon, but I'm not sure they are there yet."

C.P. was getting worried. Was he giving away too much information? Was this guy who he said he was? He was long enough in tooth, he thought, not to trust nationals. Time to move the discussion on.

"O.K. you'll have to excuse me but I've got another meeting over at the golf-club in twenty minutes, so I'll have to ask you to leave."

He heaved himself up.

"Oh, by the way, if you do limit the visas there'll be two vacant spaces in the list for mine and Doris'. I've just been asked to be Professor of Mission Studies in a University in California, and I'll be out of here in a month's time. I'll be taking all that stuff you see through there." He pointed to a vast library room through the double glass doors.

"That's twenty years of collecting books and artefacts on the Andean Republics and the history of missions. They want me to set up a centre of post-graduate studies back there in the States".

Ernesto groaned. Here was another classic example of Western Capitalism. Extract all the raw materials you can get from a country, get students from Latin America and overseas to pay vast sums for study; process the information in your own place, and then sell the products back to people who owned them in the first place!

It appeared to Ernesto that this C.P. saw his adopted country as a commodity, not as a community; a place to do business not a place to learn business; a place of personal profit, not of personal sacrifice. Maybe the country would be better without them.

"Well, thank you very much, that was very helpful, I trust that your time back in the US of A will prove to be as profitable as your time has been here."

Ernesto bowed his way out. He felt a lot more comfortable when he reached the outer patio. That was the place to be back amongst "the natives"!

• • • • • • • • • • • • • • • •

ALBERTO'S FIRST ENCOUNTER

Ernesto sat in his office and reflected on his meeting with C.P. Watkins the week before. He hadn't had time to think much about it because of the rioting in the Capital and the Provinces together with meeting after meeting among the Chiefs of Staff, the Police and members of the '*Sindicatos*', the trade unions. Food shortages were becoming an issue. Many of the little store keepers and the open markets, on which the majority of the population depended, were hoarding their stocks, fearing that imports would be restricted and that basic necessities like flour, sugar and coffee would also be restricted.

The government had imposed a ban on stockpiling flour and had created a new type of bread which would use less imported flour, a mixture of barley, quinoa, wheat flour and oats. It was proving unpopular as it was a sickly brown in colour and tasted like crushed gravel!

The government had restricted the import of vehicles to three makes, Datsun, Dodge and Volvo. They were soon to discover that Dodge trucks were not robust enough for the long grinding climbs into the Andes. Datsun pickups soon would became "rust buckets" in the humid regions of the jungle. Only the mighty Volvo could survive the taxing conditions and, though expensive, would be worth the money in the long run, The Spanish Pegaso, the Ford 600 and the Chevy pickups that had dominated the market would gradually fade away, as spares for these models were also to be limited. As for personal transport, only the VW Beetle model and its bigger brother the Combi would survive by being manufactured and imported from neighbouring Brazil.

So Ernesto's meeting with Alberto was relatively straightforward, as they continued to finalize their plan in the comparative comfort and peace of the Immigration Department Office!

"Alberto, I had a meeting with this *Jefe* mission guy and he gave me a rough idea of who the people are who are on the list and where they might be. So, I suggest you start with the ones in the highlands, then drop down to those in the jungle area, then fly back to the north coast ones and back to the city."

Ernesto passed a copy of the new list to Alberto, who took it with some reticence. This was going to be a bigger deal than he had imagined!

"Well, Colonel, *a sus órdenes* (at your service). I'll go and prepare my itinerary, collect the money from the office and be back here at the end of the month. It would be good if you give me a letter of recommendation to the various commanders of the different areas, as I'll have to lodge in some of their garrisons or maybe seek their help if I encounter any difficulties. From the reports that are coming in, things are not too stable in some of the regions. I will probably go in plain clothes in order not to spook these folks, and perhaps I'll be more able to get the information we require."

Alberto offered a sort of semi-salute, shook hands and wandered out of the room.

Back at his own flat, Alberto thought it wise to contact the *Serrano* and see if he could give him some advice about going up to the Highlands. He had never been out of the Capital, apart from the odd trip to the surfing beaches down the coast. They had kept in loose contact over the intervening years, although Alberto didn't know what he was up to or how much he was involved in any subterfuges.

He called the *Serrano* on the phone. The call eventually went through and Alberto could hear a radio blaring "*huayno*" music in the background.

"Hello", said a voice.

"Hello, it's me, Alberto, how've you been? What's going down your way?"

"Nothing much", replied the *Serrano*, "Been organising a transport strike for Friday, but you won't want to know about that, being Government now!"

"Get away with you!", Alberto replied, "But listen, I need to travel tomorrow to a place called Tambopata up in the highlands. They say there is a direct bus there?"

"Right, there will be one still tomorrow, but then the strike will be on. The company is now called '*Cooperativa 24, El Condorillu*' and its main office is in *Calle Santa Rosa* off the *Avenida La República*, but if you like you can go direct to the *Plaza Mercado Alto*, for it stops there and hangs about for passengers and the price is less than in the main office.

"It leaves about eight in the morning and you can take one piece of baggage for free. It'll go on the roof of the bus, so make sure you don't take anything you don't want stolen, and take a blanket, 'cos the heating isn't great in their buses and the bus goes up over the pass at Condormarka at 4,400 metres!

"Good Luck! Oh, by the way, there is "something else" going on up that way. Be careful who you talk to and don't ever say you are military or a policeman!"

The phone went dead.

At 7am, the next morning, Alberto took a taxi from outside his flat for the *Plaza Mercado Alto*. It took about an hour to reach his destination, due to it being rush hour, coupled with the fact that the *Plaza Mercado Alto* was across the other side of the city, on the south-east side.

The *taxista* turned out to be a lawyer, who was making a little money on the side to defray the fuel and running costs of his car. That was general practice at the moment as fuel had shot up in price in the past few weeks. Of course, there was no road tax or safety checkups on cars, but even so running costs and new cars were expensive, with a 100% import duty.

Alberto paid the driver off and stepped into the crowded plaza. There were about a dozen buses drawn up around the square, of all shapes, sizes and colours. The thing that unified them was their age and distressed condition. Some had windows missing, others had scrapes along their sides, others had their bonnets up and some were already steaming quietly in the early morning sunshine.

Their *ayudantes* (helpers) were scurrying around loading bundles and suitcases on to their roofs, all the whiles shouting "Space here for ...", whatever their final destination was.

The drivers seemed to be in the cafés around the plaza, tucking into mounds of *tallarín saltado*, or *mondongo*, seemingly unaware that they should have left some time ago! Women and boys were milling about offering sweets, chewing gum, *salteñas* and various off-coloured drinks in open bottles as remedies to combat altitude sickness.

Alberto shoved his way though the milling crowds and found himself alongside a battered bus with the letters 'Condorillu' scarcely visible on its dusty side.

"Is this the bus for Tambopata?" he asked a fat lady by its door.

"Yes, Señor, it's leaving right away. Get on board..."

"My bag?", asked Alberto. It seemed that the fat lady was the owner or conductress.

"Throw it up to the boy on the roof! The ticket is twenty dollars. Cheap, it was 25 at the bus depot!"

"Make way for the Señor", she shouted to those who were milling about just inside the bus door, selling this and that or struggling with their bags and blankets.

Alberto fished out a twenty dollar bill. The woman scratched it with her finger nail to check whether it was genuine, ripped off a small ticket from a pad, said,

"Choose any seat except the ones by the driver", and gave Alberto a gentle shove towards the steps. Alberto heaved his bag up to the boy on the roof, wondering if he would ever see it again, grabbed the rail and heaved himself into the bus. He chose a seat near the front, not that there was much choice, for most were already filled or had bags on them, but at least with this one, the leather was all in one piece and still seemed fully padded. The window beside him was secure and, apart from mud spatters, was intact.

He settled in and adjusted his blanket and woollen hat. The bus, however, failed to move in the next hour and it was nearly 10.20 am when the portly driver appeared, wiping the remains of his breakfast off his mouth with his woollen sleeve, mounted the steps and shouted,

"Let's go! "

The fat lady clambered aboard while the *ayudante* swung from the rear roof-ladder as the bus reversed slowly out through the crowd.

It would be a relatively pleasant drive down the four hundred and forty-four kilometres of tarred Pan-American highway during the heat of the rest of that day. Alberto was glad he was on the side of the bus less exposed to the sunshine and that the couple of stops were at relatively clean restaurants.

Night was beginning to fall when they arrived at the turn off for the road up into the mountains. It was a dirt road, and proved to be an incessant climb of one hundred and twenty kilometres of snaking turns to the pass at Condormarka at 4,400 metres above sea-level and thence a descent into Cachimayo before a run up the valley to Tambopata.

Before the driver set off up the hill, he pulled on another greasy pullover, a scarf and a poncho and replaced his woollen hat for a *chullu*, a local woollen hat with ear flaps. He also appeared to do something towards the rear of the bus, which a neighbour explained to Alberto. The driver was unscrewing the plugs on the silencer to allow more direct exhausting from the engine. They would lose nearly 50% of their pulling power in the thin air of the mountains. The driver also gave all the tyres a tentative kicking to ensure that there were no slow punctures.

The bus slowly roared and ground off through the gears on to the mountain road. Alberto snuggled into his blanket and attempted to sleep.

From time to time during the next few hours he would stir, adjust his cramped position and attempt to peer forward, as the headlights highlighted the rocks at times, then dark space or little puffs of swirling dust.

Once, on what must have been one of the many hairpin curves, he saw row upon row of little crosses, where a bus had plunged five hundred metres to the foaming gorge below. It would not be the last he would encounter on his journeys.

Around midnight the bus suddenly jolted to a stop! There was a banging on the door, and a dark masked figure entered, a *Sinchi*, carrying an AK40 automatic rifle.

"Get off the bus everybody! We're expecting an attack from the terrorists tonight, so you'll have to walk through the village as they may try and attack the bus. Hurry up, leave your stuff. C'mon…!"

Alberto and the rest of the passengers stepped down into the pitch dark and the rain. It was cold and miserable. With his blanket round his head, Alberto stumbled off in the dark following a wavering torch somewhere ahead. How far was this "walk"? The ground was uneven and muddy, Vague outlines of buildings appeared and disappeared in the rain and mist along the route. Five minutes passed, then ten, then twenty. Suddenly the light stopped and people bumped into each other in a soggy, grumbling huddle.

Behind them they heard the bus coming up in the distance and eventually saw its small coloured side lights gradually coming nearer through the mist and the rain. 'Almost Christmaslike', Alberto thought, although Christmas was to be banned this year as it smacked of Western Imperialism and Santa was to be replaced by an Inca folk figure, and llamas for reindeer!

They scrambled aboard, damp and cold. The bus's heating was minimal and the door had been open all the time so that driver could leap off if the firing started.

"*Así es la vida* (such is life)" said his neighbour and offered him a swig from a hip flask and Alberto huddled down in an attempt to sleep again.

He came to after some time as the bus seemed to be going a little faster now and with downhill motion, the bus's exhaust popping and banging and the transmission whining a lower gear.

Another hour passed for Alberto in this semi-stupor when again the bus ground to a halt.

"It's the Cachimayo bridge… We have to walk over it"

"Why is that? Terrorists here again?"

"No, they've left the area, but the bridge is damaged and inclined at an angle of twenty degrees, so there's a chance that a loaded bus might topple into the river!"

Alberto was glad when all this business of walking over a drunken bridge was at an end and the bus started on its final stretch up into the town of Tambopata where the Macdonald couple lived. He hoped there might be a decent hotel where he could get cleaned up, have a meal and get into drier clothes before setting off to find them.

Alberto's hopes were only semi-fulfilled. The Hotel Dorado, in the plaza opposite the bus office, was golden in colour but dreary in service and facilities. He did get a plate of watery soup with the odd spaghetti floating in it and coriander flavouring, coffee and bread, and he did get a room whose window did not fully close; the toilet tank was bereft of a cover so that he had to fish in it to release the flushing mechanism, but at least the bed looked good. He dozed the early hours away and prepared himself to go out around late morning.

The town itself was busy, the stores and commercial businesses looked semi-prosperous and there was little sign of military presence. He looked for the post-office where he thought that they might give directions to the Macdonalds' place.

The post-office was under a colonnade at the corner of the square. The bespectacled clerk behind the counter, with watery eyes and a droopy moustache, eyed him closely.

"How can I serve you?" he asked politely.

"I'm look for some *gringos* called Macdonald",

"Ah, of course, you mean, Don Donaldo, *Pato* Donaldo (Donald Duck). A fine person, he comes in most days, but he lives a couple of blocks down from the plaza, number 204, Constitution Street. You can't miss it, just before the Evangelical Church. He and his wife, the Señora Shona, have lived here for many years."

Alberto set off down the cobbled Constitution Street. It was nice to feel the hot sun on his back even although the air was chilly. He came across the small house, number 204, with its iron railings and a small garden filled with geraniums, a bougainvillea in one corner, a jacaranda tree in the other. He was surprised that the iron railing gate was open, so he went forward and knocked on the front door of the house.

"*Pase no más!* (Just come in!)", called a woman's voice from somewhere within. Alberto hesitated, this would never happen in the capital, where everyone lived behind high walls, guard dogs, cameras and electric or barbed wire fencing!

"*Disculpe Señora, una preguntita, por favor* (Excuse me, lady, just a question please)", called Alberto.

A lady appeared in the hallway. She was small, with a round rosy face and pigtails. She was dressed in a skirt and thick patterned sweater and her hands were covered in what appeared to be flour.

"How can I help you?" she enquired, in Spanish, with a smile.

"I am from the Ministry of Immigration in the capital and I need to ask you some questions as to what you are doing here? It's part of our new checkup on immigrants and their visa situation".

"Oh, you poor soul, you look tired. Come on in and have a cup of something; my husband will be in in a moment. I'm just teaching our maid how to make *torta de limón* (lemon sponge-cake). She wants to make them for her mother to sell on her stall in the market."

Alberto was intrigued that this couple would need a maid, but he was gratified that they seemed to treat her more as a daughter than a skivvy.

The house appeared to have just two rooms, a big lounge/diner and a bedroom. The kitchen seemed to be in a separate building in the yard at the back. Alberto glanced around and sat down on a hard chair as the woman went off through to the back.

He noticed that on the dresser there were some photos of young *'gringos'* and other family groups, across from a large bookcase full of books and papers and what appeared to be a book on the table with the title *Santa Biblia* (Holy Bible). Alberto knew little about Christianity, let alone missionary work, so he thought the presence of the Bible to be something quite odd.

There was a noise at the front door and in walked a tall tanned man with an athletic step and balding hair. It was don Donaldo.

"Hi there, *mi estimado*, (my esteemed one). I am don Donaldo and whom do I have the pleasure of meeting here?"

Alberto introduced himself and at that moment Shona came through with some cake and coffee.

She offered it to Alberto first and then to Donaldo.

"We always like to give God thanks for His provision for us", she said hastily before Alberto could take a bite.

Alberto didn't know what to do, but Donaldo said simply,

"Thank you, God, for this opportunity to meet don Alberto and for this food, in the name of Jesus, Amen!"

Alberto liked the cake and the welcome smile on their faces.

"Tell me", said Alberto, as he was finishing the cake, "what do you do here?"

"Well, you name it, we do it!" laughed Donaldo.

"I've just come in from fixing the generating plant in the market.

The motor kept overheating... It's one of the new generating sets that have come from Russia and all the manuals are in Russian, so it took a bit of figuring out what the problem was and it turned out that the thermostat on the cooling system was installed upside down and was closing off the water supply to the motor instead of opening it up when the engine warmed up! I used to be a mechanic before God called me to be a missionary to your country."

"He's always fixing things for others", said his wife with a smile, "but he could do with fixing our leaking kitchen roof!"

"Well, my beloved, we'll get there one day!" They both laughed.

"Yes", continued Alberto, "but what are you actually here for? Surely there are lots of national mechanics and cooks around, are there not?"

"Of course! But as Christians we have to serve others as well as tell folks the Good News that Jesus died on the cross for their sins and can transform their lives."

"And this 'Good-News' makes a difference to people, does it?"

"Well, you'd have to ask the folks that form part of the little church here that. We have about one hundred and fifty or so who worship regularly in the building next door that they built with their own hands.

"Take Rogelio for example. He was the town drunk, one of them at least! One night, he was coming home from a fiesta and he heard a group of us singing a Christian song here in the house. He rolled in, Shona plonked him down in a corner and he listened to what I was saying to the folks about God's love to all that were gathered here. He says he fell asleep and God spoke to him and said, 'Rogelio, I want to give you a new life'. When he woke up in the morning, he was stone cold sober, and from that day, three years ago, he's a new man and now has begun to work as a porter in the market and tell others about what God has done for him."

"Interesting", mused Alberto, "and, have you had any problems while you've been here, say with the military, the terrorists or the Roman Catholics or the communists?"

Donaldo was slow to reply.

"Where does one begin?" He glanced across at his wife and then looked Alberto straight in the eye and gripped his arm.

"Well, don Alberto, to be frank with you, there used to be problems with the priest here. He was from the group called *Opus Dei* and he thought that we were heretics! He encouraged the people not to speak to us when we first came fifteen years ago. He said that our Bible", pointing to the book on the table, "was false, even although the translation dated from 1603, and that nobody had the right to read or understand the Word of God, only the priest. He and others set fire to the building we were in one night, having locked the door from the outside, and it was by the grace of God that we were able to smash a window and get out before the roof caved in. But, after some months, his own house caught fire in an accident with his paraffin cooker in the kitchen and he was made homeless!

"We, as a group, went round and helped him rebuild it. He has never bothered us since.

"Furthermore, we have never had any problems from the terrorists. I am a Quechua speaker and I work most of my time in the *"campo"* (rural areas). They know that we have worked in literacy projects and in the revitalisation of Quechua music, the use of native musical instruments and native hymnology. When the big earthquake occurred in the region of Mullupampa and Soccllapata, we organised relief through *Tear Fund* and other international aid agencies.

"The terrorists, although we don't agree with them, are in some ways up for social justice in a way that, if you'll pardon the assertion, your government hasn't been!

"For example, the terrorists came into the village of Iscaywasi last year and asked the villagers if the *comerciantes* (traders) were being honest in buying their potato crop and selling other goods to those in the community. They also asked if anyone was committing adultery or child-molesting. If there were such folks around, the terrorists promised to come back in three weeks and shoot them all! They came back three weeks later, and were told that one *comerciante*'s scales were doctored and that three men in the village had been abusing children. The terrorists took the culprits out into the plaza and shot them then and there!"

Alberto didn't know what to say. Life obviously was a little more complicated than the mere Marxist rhetoric he had been accustomed to in the groups in the pubs or universities in the capital.

"Where are you going from here?" Señora Shona asked.

"Well, I have to visit several others, but I have the name of a family Penner who live in the next *Departamento* (county) in a place called Amrasmarka"

"Oh, yes, we know them well. They are not in our missionary society and they work with a different Quechua dialect group but they are fine people. You'll like them and they have their kids with them, I think; they were home schooling them. Our children are gone now. Our boy is in Scotland studying to be an engineer. He would like to come back here though."

Alberto noticed that the Señora had gone very quiet and sad and was that tears in her eyes?

"Yes," said Donaldo slowly, "we had a girl too, Mary is her name, but she died here when she was nine. She was bitten by a scorpion, and she was allergic to penicillin and we didn't know it. We couldn't bury her in the local cemetery as it was only for Catholics, so we buried her on a friend's farm outside the town. It's now a little evangelical cemetery."

Alberto remembered his mother. At last he said,

"Well, thank you very much. It has been a pleasure to talk to you. I don't foresee any problems with your renewal. If you come to the Capital, please ask for me personally in the Immigration Department, so that I can facilitate you. Here is my card."

He rose and shook hands with the couple and marched quickly out of the door

"*Hasta la vista* (until the next time)" they called after him, from the gate.

ALBERTO'S SECOND ENCOUNTER

The journey to the Penners proved a little less eventful than the initial one. The *colectivo* (12-seater mini-bus) was quicker and a little more comfortable than the inter-provincial bus had been. It was almost too quick for Alberto's liking, sitting as he was on the front-seat bench, "the suicide seat", as some people called it. There were no seat-belts in the vehicle and he knew that, in a head-on crash, he would either be flattened like a pancake or catapulted into eternity.

The little Virgin Mary and the woolly dice swung to and fro in front of his nose like some hypnotist's gadget and the *chofercillu* (driver) talked incessantly over his shoulder to the *ayudante* behind him, about football, women, all the other bad drivers, the cost of fuel and the lousy government, interspersed with curses and swearing at slower vehicles in his way.

It was two hours to the next town that had a railway station. There, still aching from adjusting his position continually round the snaking curves, he made his way to the station. The trains left here twice a day for the south of the country, over the high rolling '*puna*', the Andean plains, at eleven thousand feet above sea level.

Alberto could make out an old *Garrat* steam locomotive beyond the station platform. Those had been designed years before to deal with the tight curves on some of the sections of the Andean lines. It hissed and fussed in the engine yard behind. Alberto hoped that today's train would be hauled by one of the newer diesel locomotives, part of Great Britain's last stand as a railway giant and the country that had been responsible nearly a century before for the building of most railways in South America. Sure enough, there it was waiting for him, a gleaming 1955 *Metrovic Class 22* loco at the head of some 1920-30's carriages and goods wagons.

Alberto settled himself into a second-class compartment, refused the offer of a cup of *mate de coca* (coca leaf infused tea) and munched reflectively on a large sandwich of ham, chicken and cheese. Two hours would see him into the town of Santa Barbara, a hotel and a night's rest before tackling the Penners in Amrasmarka

However, as the saying goes, *"Entre dicho y hecho hay mucho trecho"*, (Many a slip 'twixt cup and lip!). The station tannoy blared some incomprehensible message that echoed round the hills, to the effect that the train would be delayed for several hours as the inbound train from the south had been derailed, due to *un pequeño disperfecto* (a little fault), but literally due to sabotage!

The train did leave eventually as dark was closing in and soon reached its maximum speed of fifteen miles an hour, so it was dark when Alberto reached his destination. There were several moto-taxis awaiting the train's arrival and Alberto commandeered one and asked to be taken to the best hotel in town. He had a good sense of direction and it soon appeared to him that his driver was taking a very long way round for a shortcut. Alberto poked him in the back and shouted in his ear,

"Oye, flaco, soy militar. Ponte las pilas y llévame al hotel (Listen, skinny, I'm a member of the military. Get a grip and take me where I want to go)!"

The *taxista* swerved down an alley which brought Alberto up to the entrance of the *Hotel Turista*. Alberto haggled over the fare, paid only half what the *taxista* demanded and went inside the hotel. He would set off in the morning to find the Penners.

It was a beautiful frosty morning and the peaks of *Apu Salkantáy* and *Apu Ausangate* stood white and shining in the thin atmosphere as a background to the market and the taxi rank. Alberto had the Penners' address that seemed to be a Bible Institute of sorts about five kilometres out of town.

After a series of haggling, he squeezed into a battered VW Beetle whose back mudguards were wired through the body and across the back seat. There were no mirrors and the rear window was covered by a piece of opaque plastic and duck-tape. The windscreen was cracked and he noticed that the front main headlamps were wired on. They seemed to be a "must-have" for thieves all over the country at the moment!

The twenty minute journey was noisy and dusty- noise from the motor, noise from the radio and from the unpaved road surface. He refrained from speaking to the *taxista* who provided a noisy commentary on politics, women and the economy. Alberto had heard this referred to as "taxicology", the "science" that taxi drivers knew all about everything!

The Bible Institute in Amrasmarka stood in an open area surrounded by fields of maize and barley. The adjacent houses and what looked like a dormitory block were mud-brick built and showed signs of ageing.

Alberto rang a metal triangle of construction rod that served as a bell. A tall man with greying hair appeared. It was Leslie Penner.

"Hi, how can I help you?" He said smiling and shaking Alberto's outstretched hand

Alberto went through his speech about who he was and why he was there and the pair moved into a patio where they sat down in a couple of bamboo chairs.

"Sorry my wife, Jodie, isn't around; she and my daughter Brenda are taking our son, John, who's seventeen, to the airport today. He's on his way to Winnipeg to study his final grades and enter the flying programme there. He wants to be a pilot."

Alberto thought to himself, where do they get the money for a programme like that?

Almost as if Leslie had read his mind, he volunteered:

"It's taken all our savings and help from several grant foundations for "mish" kids to get him into that. But then, heh, if you don't sacrifice for your kids, what's life all about? And we do believe as Christians that God will provide. Look around at this place, no government money, just pure prayer, sweat and tears over the years."

Alberto didn't know how to reply. He just grunted. Then he moved on to ask what was taught here.

"Oh, lots of courses… theology, practical preaching, open-air work, radio preaching, and practical courses like motor mechanics, carpentry, construction, photography, so that local village preachers and evangelists can support themselves until a church is formed who will then take them on as full-time pastors. Also a number of us here are involved in translation and literacy work."

"Translation work, what's that?" asked Alberto.

"Well the Bible has been around in Spanish since 1569, but most folks round here have Quechua or Aymara as their mother tongue. Some are still monolingual while most people now are bi-lingual, and your government is going to start a programme of initial literacy in people's mother tongue. Did you know Quechua is spoken by about twelve million people in the Andean Republics and it has some seven dialects and some are mutually exclusive? So there's quite a bit to be done still!"

"To me, these tribal languages must be very limited in expression, not like Spanish, 'the language of love'," Alberto chipped in.

Leslie laughed outright! "You couldn't be more wrong. Quechua is a fascinating language. Take, for example this one line of a hymn:'*Wajllay cruzpi Cristo ñakaripullawarqa…*' Quechua is a suffix-adding language, so you get 'Our dear, Christ on the cross..', then 'ñaka-ri-pu-lla-wa-rqa', ñaka = to suffer; ri = over and over again; pu = for my benefit; lla = yes indeed; wa = for me; rqa = an action in the past, with results in the present, He did it! Pretty good, for just one word, eh?"

"I never knew it was so complex!" admitted Alberto.

"Tell you what, don Alberto, if you are doing nothing special for the next couple of days, why don't you come with me on a trip up into the mountains. I have to go and visit a couple of lady missionaries, Mary Brown and Jessica Short, who work out in the sticks there, and you'll get a flavour of how tough these girls are and what a great job they do in an area where there is little medical attention. I have to take some supplies up to them. It's about a seven hour trip from here."

Alberto suddenly realised that these were another two names on the list so he could *matar dos pájarros con un solo tiro* (kill two birds with one stone).

"Well, if it's not too much bother", he replied gratefully.

"No, it would be great, because my co-worker, don Alejandro Vílchez, who is sixty-five, is bothered with his rheumatism this week and can't come. He used to walk from village to village all over this area, preaching and teaching the word of God. He was stoned, imprisoned for it, when he was young, but he is a father figure in this area, respected and listened to by all and sundry. He preaches now on the radio in Quechua every day for an hour on *Radio Popular 200* and sings the hymns he has composed, for the many new congregations in the rural areas to learn by heart.

"Would you give me a hand then to load the pick-up, then we'll have a bite to eat and get going? Don't want to be doing too much of the drive in the dark!"

The pick-up was a 4WD grey *Chevvy 300*, with an old '*Montana,*

Big-Sky Country' plate on the back but national plates on the front and the relevant numbers painted on the sides. It was already loaded with two 50 gallon drums of fuel, a full 20 gallon tank, two spare wheels and a heavy tool box. Alberto helped throw in two 50 kilo sacks of flour, one of sugar, an 18 gallon drum of kerosene, a bundle of blankets, two sleeping bags, a sack of bread, a box with cans of beans, evaporated milk, canned butter and jam, medical supplies, a pick, two shovels, a crowbar and a length of heavy chain.

"Put these thermos flasks in the cab, don Alberto. I've just got this stainless steel one recently, can't think how many of the glass ones I've bust on trips. Hope you like country-western music, my friend has just given me a new cassette!"

The first 20 kilometres or so were on a gravelled highway, so they bowled along in the noonday sunshine. People were working in the fields and Alberto was amazed at the complex irrigation systems in the valley, a heritage from the Inca Empire. Then they turned off and headed up a steep narrow dirt road leaving a huge plume of dust in their wake.

"We can only do about fifteen kilometres an hour "max" on this road. Had a lot of rain earlier this year and the grader hasn't been over it yet!"

Alberto was already bouncing up and down on the bench seat and had already cracked his head twice on the roof of the cab.

"Best stick your elbow out the window to brace yourself and watch the road not the scenery!" Les laughed, as he wound the wheel back and forth.

The road itself snaked up the face of the mountain until they came to a level spot and a small village. The dogs and chickens scattered at they roared through it. The silencer on the pickup was non existent.

"Not very popular here. The other month I killed a goat in the road here by mistake, Took an hour to haggle over its cost. But we had meat for a day or two after!"

They continued on up to the *Huayraccasa* pass at 4,420 meters above sea level.

There, at the top by the side of the road, were two large cairn-like piles of stones, and an old gnarled wooden cross. Les pulled over for a moment and motioned to Alberto to come over to look more closely at one stone pile. Alberto was feeling a bit light headed so he gingerly made his way over the rough ground to the pathway between the stones.

"See what's here," said Les, as he poked among the rocks and came up with several coins, a dirty piece of cloth and a lock of twisted horse-hair.

"This is an *apachita*. Folks believe that the spirit of the mountain needs an offering for you to pass over its top. You can give a drink offering to *Pacha Mama* (Mother Earth) who is here too to take away your *Pacha jap'iskqa* (altitude sickness); or you can leave a piece of clothing from your sickbed or bandage and transfer the sickness, your *soq'a wayra jap'isqa* to the winds up here; or you can undo a curse by leaving something twisted with a left-handed twist; then you can pray at the cross and leave a candle. Frankly, I usually take the money for bread for folks in the village at home, and the candles for their houses!"

"Don't you believe in the spirits then?" asked Alberto.

"Oh, yes, I do! I've seen too much of what the *paqos, hampiris, carisiris, watoqs, hampeqs* and other shamans can do not to believe, but I can also see the power of God's Holy Spirit that can outdo anything they might be able to do. Yes, sir! Let's go, then!"

They set off down the sixty-five hairpins to the valley bottom, two thousand metres below, as the sun dipped behind the *Apu Pisti* volcanic peak. In the dusk they crossed the narrow Pachachaca bridge, with the river swirling in the gorge below, and started up the other side to the next crest. They passed the shattered remains of a truck sticking out of the rocks in the river.

"They missed the bridge corner, last spring. Forty-five people coming from a Fiesta, they and their driver were all stone-drunk after three days of it. The driver survived the fall into the gorge but filled his pockets with stones, and threw himself into the river and was drowned."

Things were going as well as could be expected on such roads until they began the final descent towards the village of Qoribamba where the two women lived. Les skidded to a halt, when round a curve they came on a rock fall with a little bushy tree in the centre of the road waving quietly at them in the evening mountain breezes!

"Let's see what the damage is..." and Les slid out of the cab. It was mainly loose dry earth and boulders and the little tree. To the right the ground sloped steeply upwards and still looked quite unstable. To the left the road dropped sharply away in the growing darkness to the valley below.

"I suppose we'll have to go back or wait for a bulldozer, if there is one somewhere," mused Alberto.

"Well, the folks are waiting for these supplies and it's two hours walk still down to the village, so we just have to get on with it and see if we can clear enough to squeeze past".

Alberto eyed the drop and gulped. He didn't fancy getting close to the edge. Les brought the tools and began shovelling and kicking rocks and soil over the drop.

After an hour of steady work between them, by the light of the headlamps, they had cleared enough to perhaps just squeeze past, save for one drawback, a branch of the tree that stuck its arm out like a traffic cop.

"I've got my little axe somewhere in the toolkit, but it'll take a while to chop through that!"

It took another half an hour of chopping and hacking in the dark to snap it off.

Les threw the tools in the back of the pickup, jumped in, engaged the 4WD and inched forward in low gear.

"You walk past the gap and advise me if it's a goer, or not", he told Alberto.

Alberto tip-toed past the slide and through the gap. He waved Les forward. The near-side front wheel grazed the rocks, causing small stones to start to slide down again, the far-side front wheel was inches from the drop. Les inched forward...

"¡Suave no más, suave! (Gently does it, gently!)" Alberto gesticulated wildly.

The front wheels cleared the fall and Les rushed the back ones through the gap as the stones began to fall again and the edge began to crumble.

"Thank you, Lord, thank you," Les cried, wiping the sweat and dust off his forehead. "Well, we're here, though when we'll get back is another matter!"

Forty minutes later they swung into the plaza of Qoribamba and saw a faint light in the house of the two missionaries in the street below the plaza. It was nine-thirty pm. Les banged on the door.

"Hi there folks, can you open the big gate and we'll park up in the barn. I guess the two bunks in there are empty. Don't worry about us, we'll talk in the morning, I've got a friend from the coast with me".

Jessica came out with a *Petromax* kerosene lantern and opened the gate and barn door for them.

She looked pretty haggard herself as she had just walked back in the afternoon from another village, three hours away, where she had been delivering a baby.

"Okay, see you tomorrow, breakfast here at 6.00am. Busy day with a clinic tomorrow", she added.

The men drove the pickup into the barn, took out the blankets, thermos and sleeping bags, then used the hole-in-the floor toilet and "hit the pit".

Alberto could hear Les, muttering below him, perhaps he was praying again. Then he fell asleep.

They were woken with a start by a cock crowing and jumping down on the box beside them. It was five-thirty in the morning. There was no water in the barn, so they scrubbed their faces as best they could and went over to the house. Mary was busy at the kerosene stove over a pot of what looked like porridge and Jessica was just putting her Bible and prayer list on a shelf when they entered.

'Good mornings', were made all around as Les introduced Alberto to the two ladies. Breakfast was a bowl of porridge and a mug of sweet coffee. Alberto noticed that his mug had the words '*Sup up, say nowt*' on it, whatever that meant.

Things started happening - noises outside indicated that a queue was beginning to form to see the nurses, a roar in the background suggested that the village bulldozer was starting up and setting off on its slow journey up to the rockfall, and inside, the large kettle for boiling the water to ensure clean drinking water started spitting over the stove.

"We must get on, too", Les said, his chair scraping on the uneven concrete floor. "We'll unload the stuff, and follow the tractor up. Sorry we can't stay for a chat, and to hear how the work is going, but we'll see you next week when you come down to us for a day or two. Our Brenda loves having a time with her "aunties" and doing these girlie things!"

Alberto saw what a tight knit and caring community these missionary folks were, yet so open also to the community at large.

"We'll stop in the plaza and see if anyone needs a lift, though I expect there might be other trucks going out today as well. I saw the big *cerveza* (beer) one was parked up last night. The bus isn't due in until Friday, I guess."

They shook hands, hugged and got ready to go and while doing so Mary prayed, asking God's blessing on them all and strength for the day's tasks. Alberto thought she had such a lovely quiet voice. He would have liked to get to know her better. She must have been about his age, he thought. Maybe one day, when she comes to the Capital for her visa. He wondered why such a slim and attractive girl would lose herself in a place like this.

The journey back was relatively uneventful, except that Les decided to visit two miners working their own silver mine another hundred meters up beyond the top of the pass. They climbed up a narrow path from the road to the mine entrance and Alberto checked that his pulse was doing 130bpm when he arrived there, out of breath. The two miners were sitting over a small stove with a can of coffee on it. They were dirty, bearded and their clothes, ponchos and caps all seemed to be of the same grey-black colour as themselves and the piles of stone around them.

They smiled through uneven yellow teeth, as Les approached.

"Allinllachu waukikuna, (Hello brothers)", Les greeted them.

"Allinmi, waukillay (We're well, my brother)", they replied.

Alberto was not able to follow what followed; not only was the Spanish "funny" with vowels and the stress on many words changed to Quechua intonation patterns, but half the conversations were in Quechua as well!

On the way back down, Les explained that these two miners were following a silver vein into the mountain and that they spent a month at a time sleeping up there and reading the Bible in their spare time. They would be coming to the Bible Institute in June for a month when it was too cold and snowy to work the mine up there. They sold their quartz ore to a small mining outfit and then for the rest of their time they went back down to the coast where they had small houses and families.

Alberto began to wonder what all this had to do with the Revolution, the coast or the Capital's way-of-life! All these places so far had been other worlds, a million miles away from his own life and from the country as it was portrayed by the Government or the Tourist Boards. Maybe his next visit would be more "normal".

• •

ALBERTO'S THIRD ENCOUNTER

Alberto was sorry to leave the Penners. They had been more than kind to him and accepted him for who he was. Why, they had even prayed for him!

He had made his way to the airport in the highland city, a mecca for tourists and an international gateway. He was looking for a flight of some sort to get him down into the jungle area of the Eastern slopes of the Andes. That's where his next group of missionaries were to be found. Trouble was, he discovered that there was no direct flight to that area, it seemed. Flashing his official badge, he wandered over to the area where several smaller aircraft were parked and asked around about flights to the Amazon basin area.

A mechanic pointed his greasy rag to an ex military Russian *Antenov* type of aircraft over to the left.

"That one flies to Santa Rosa, San Juan del Mayo and other strips down that way, once a week. It's been delayed due to an engine fault but it's more or less okay now and will be going this afternoon. Ask in the office over there".

Alberto entered the small wooden hut that served as an office for military flights and, showing his credentials, asked the clerk if there might be the possibility of a seat on the flight in the afternoon.

The clerk laughed out loud!

"A seat? This is a cargo plane, but you can sit around in it if you like! Be back here at 1pm" He stamped a small ticket-like piece of paper and handed it to Alberto.

Alberto wandered over to the plane. It had a sort of ramp entrance in the tail, a high wing configuration with two small turboprop engines, long spindly undercarriage struts and smallish double landing wheels. He was alarmed to see that a couple of the wheels were down to their canvas core in parts; there also seemed to be a bit of an oil leak from one of the motors and several rivets had popped on the leading edge of the tail section. The belly and underside of its tail section were heavily mud spattered.

Returning after a light snack in the airport café (better not to eat too much in a rock and roll, un-pressurised flight, down over the Andes!), he was surprised to see that they were finished loading and that the plane had been towed out to the take-off area. There were only two other passengers, as well as a couple of cargo handlers. The passengers were a lady and a little girl about seven years of age, the captain's family, he was told.

Alberto settled himself midway up the hold beside one of the small porthole windows and the lady and child sat opposite on folding canvas seats, beside the cargo nets. The plane's ramp flap slowly closed and semi-darkness set in. There were only small emergency lights in the hold. The noise was loud and irritating, a combination of roaring and whining. They had estimated the flight time to be about an hour or so, depending on the weather.

Then they were soon up and off and through the small window Alberto caught a glimpse of a mountainside dipping away from them. Then, nothing but clear sky and the occasional puffy white cloud. The plane did tend to jump and wallow from time to time. Obviously it was having an effect on the little girl. Her mother produced a transparent plastic bag and the little girl obligingly filled it with the contents of what must have been her breakfast and lunch.

Not a pretty sight!

One of the cargo handlers took the "contribution", unscrewed a small flap in the side of the fuselage and emptied the contents over over some mountain or village!

Alberto began to see glimpses of greenery rather than rock and mountain. He detected the plane was decreasing in height and velocity and his ears began to pop. The little girl was crying and complaining that her ears hurt and her mother was telling her to keep swallowing.

Soon dense forest appeared, wreathed in mist.

Then, without warning, the ramp, the rear section of the plane, began to open! Alberto began to find himself staring into a void some one hundred metres above the forest floor, as the plane banked sharply towards its run in to the grassy five hundred metre landing strip at Santa Rosa.

Slowly the earth and the wheels neared each other. Would the impact on bare canvas rupture the tyre? The jolt was greater than he expected and he was thrown to the floor, madly grabbing the netting lest he be sucked out the back.

The child howled in fear as her mother held her with one hand and crossed herself with the other. Another jolt as the engines roared in reverse and the brakes were slammed on in order to come to a shuddering halt just short of the end of the runway and the river. They taxied back to the small building that served as office, waiting room and baggage area. It seemed almost beatific to Alberto!

He thought that it would be better (safer?) to go by road for the rest of the way. The former President, despite all the things the Revolution had said about him, had begun to establish *rutas de penetración* (highways) into the Eastern Andes Region. Most of them were unfinished, but some areas were now interconnected. It would be good to try it anyway. He had a fear that the plane might not make the next stage. He had heard rumours too that pilots would suddenly claim plane faults in order to spend a day or two at a fiesta or go hunting, shooting or fishing in the jungle!

Alberto cast about for a taxi or a local bus, but eventually settled for a Land Rover, owned by a local business man who was going to the main town where the mission group were and where the mission hospital was. It turned out that he was actually going to the hospital himself to have his eyes operated on as he was losing his sight!

"Oh, yes, there is an amazing Megan Jenkins there that does this operation, much better than the ones in the Capital and it's cheaper too!"

They set off down *La Marginal* (the Highway). The Land Rover chugged and rattled along at a dignified thirty kilometres an hour leaving a plume of dust and, with the windows slid back, there was a cool and refreshing breeze on Alberto's face.

The business man, Arquitecto Miguel Alvarado Linares, reminisced on the way.

"Ten years ago all this area was virgin jungle. There were all sorts of animals and birds here, but the government, after the road was put in, decided that they wanted to increase the amount of palm oil that the country exported, so they cleared this thirty kilometre stretch and a couple of kilometres deep either side of the road, to plant a palm oil plantation. The oil was never going to be processed here but the nuts were to be shipped down rivers to a processing plant in Brazil. Since that time, the price of palm oil on the world market dropped and so it's not really viable. Some folks are cutting bits of the plantation down and growing cocaine, but I'm not supposed to tell you that!

"You see, cocaine gives you four harvests a year, palm oil only one. And it's easily processed locally and then flown out to Colombia for refining. This will be the main crop in all this area soon and you'll have to work it or get out. Actually you military, I believe, are sanctioning this, and protecting the "narcos", but heh, what do I know?.

"I'm moving to the Capital at the end of the year when I get my eyes fixed. There's no future here beyond the drug business. And, the terrorists are beginning to take over from the military in controlling the drug trade. We're beginning to see bodies coming downstream of people who didn't want to work cocaine or didn't want to give up their land for cocaine. It's becoming a world within a world".

Great splodges of raindrops suddenly appeared on the windscreen, the sky darkened and visibility dropped to almost zero.

"It looks like if it might rain", said the businessman laughingly.

The noise of the rainfall was deafening and the dusty road became a muddy stream in less than thirty seconds. There was a crack of thunder and a great flash of chain lightning careered across the bonnet of the vehicle.

The businessman fiddled the Land Rover into 4WD and ploughed slowly forward. It was hard to see where the road actually was, it was more like being at sea!

Just as suddenly as the cloudburst had started, so the rain stopped and the sun appeared through a rift in the clouds. Conditions changed again. Now it was a steaming mist that floated at knee height, making the muddy road invisible. and leaving the trees standing out like sentinels on either side.

The Land Rover's wheels suddenly began to rotate at speed but the body of the vehicle remained still.

"Ay, *carambas,* we're in a mudhole!" exclaimed the businessman. He looked out of the door and saw that all four wheels were firmly lodged in a sea of mud. Revving the engine was only digging them deeper.

"One has to be prepared for this", he said phlegmatically.

Hopping out in the mud, he made his way round to the front of the Land Rover and started to unwind the cable of the power winch. Dragging the cable, he hitched it round the nearest strong sapling and ploughed his way back again.

"O.K., let's give it a go..."

He engaged the winch and at the same time put the vehicle into double low 4WD. The Land Rover shivered like a wild salmon on a hook but slowly emerged from the mud-hole on to firmer ground.

"*Pan de cada día,* (Same old story)", he moaned, "I don't expect these roads will ever get asphalted in my lifetime".

They continued snaking their way towards the town, passing a couple of trucks and a bus, all bogged down at the soft edges of the road.

"Sorry, *amigos,* another day perhaps", as he waved jauntily at their predicaments.

The businessman dropped Alberto off at the end of the track into the hospital and mission compound. Alberto thanked him profusely and wondered how people managed to survive in these primitive conditions.

A battered notice read '*Hospital Evangélico, San Juan del Mayo*'. In his muddy shoes, Alberto walked down the track and through a large archway into a grassy area with a netball court, a large mango tree and three or four tamped earth buildings with red pan-tiled roofs.

Two fair-haired little children were playing there in the muddy puddles making mud pies. A lady's head popped out of the half-door, calling,

"Don't let little Debbie get too muddy, Robert!"

Alberto wondered if this was the Burns family from Australia.

"Hello", he shouted and waved. The head disappeared for a moment, the bottom half of the door opened, the lady ran out, scooped up the children and disappeared inside!

Then, a small bespectacled man appeared at the door and said in faltering Spanish,

"*¿Qué cosa quiere Usted.? No es hospital aquí.* (What do you want? This isn't the hospital),"and pointed back up the track.

Alberto spoke slowly, loudly and carefully,

"I am Lieutenant Colonel Alberto Sánchez from the Immigration Service in the Capital, and I have come myself to interview the family Burns, the family Jenkins and the family De Groots. At your service, Meester".

"*Un momento*", replied the young man and he closed the doors and also disappeared.

Several minutes later, the door half opened again and an oldish man with white hair and half spectacles appeared.

"Good afternoon, I am Doctor Daniel Jenkins, the hospital director and surgeon. I understand you wish to interview us. Please come in and I am arranging for all such persons to be present here in a moment or two. I see you are quite muddy, so would you be kind enough to leave your shoes at the door and I will get someone to clean them for you. Do you take tea or coffee? We normally have tea on the balcony here at four, but it is a little early for that, so we will have it now in the salon".

Alberto noted that he spoke very good Spanish without much of a foreign accent, if a little literary in its style. He left his shoes at the door and moved into a large airy room with a tiled floor, ceiling fan and shuttered, glassless windows covered in mosquito netting. The wooden chairs were of local construction, probably, he thought, of mahogany from the area around them.

Gradually the room filled up with the "suspects" and a local Indian girl brought in a tray full of cups, plates, a large teapot, sugar and milk, while another of the party brought in a large sponge cake and a knife.

"Let me introduce everybody", said Doctor Daniel. "This is my wife Megan, a nurse mid-wife but also likes to do operations…! To be honest, she hasn't the paper qualifications but ask anyone east of the Andes and they will say they prefer her to me!"

There was a ripple of laughter round the room, although Alberto could see that Mrs Burns was struggling to follow the conversation in Spanish, as well as wrestling with the two bored children.

"Then those over there are Hans and Nelly De Groot from Holland who have come to help in the Bible Institute that is over there in that building behind you. They have recently come from language learning in Costa Rica and are getting used to the local dialect here, which you will have noticed is quite different from the way folks in Costa Rica or the Capital speak!"

Again there was a ripple of laughter and someone said in a low voice "¡A Tashaw. De verasmente! (Oh my goodness me! Indeed!)"

The Burns and the De Groots looked blank.

"How can we help you, then?"

Alberto wasn't sure how to proceed. He had hoped to see them all individually in their homes and their ministries, but here it was eight to one, if you included the children.

"Well..." and then began a long introductory discourse about the Revolution, it aims and its values, etc. After several minutes, he could see that he had lost the Burns, who had turned their attention to their restless kids, and the De Groots who had had enough of Revolutions etc. with Apartheid in South Africa and the Gay Rights movement in Holland, only the Señora Megan seemed at all interested in what he was saying. So he drew to a close and finished by saying,

"So I am here to see how your aims and methods are in accord with the aims and values of the Revolution. Any questions?"

The silence was deafening and people squirmed uncomfortably on their chairs and stared at the wall and ceiling. That is all, save the Señora. Megan.

"Tell me", she said, "what are you going to do about bringing proper medical attention to this area? You realise that we, as a mission, have been here as a hospital since 1932, when the first two English nurses came by mule into this area over the Andes from the coast, and set up a clinic here. Since then we have treated thousands of men and women and brought not only physical healing but also spiritual healing to them. That has transformed this area and now there are little self supporting, self governing and self propagating churches all over this area.

Our hospital has also trained scores of nursing staff for the new hospital in the big town and districts. But my husband is still operating on a First World War second-hand operating table and now the Burns family have just arrived because he is an engineer and we hope to install a 40 KW. generating set for the hospital and area around. I think that is all part of a Revolution. What is your revolution going to do for us here, Teniente?"

Megan's eyes shone brightly and her cheeks were quite flushed. She had spoken with the fire of the old Welsh Chapel preachers that were in her blood.

Alberto suddenly felt that this was his mother addressing him again! He cleared his throat noisily and started,

"Well... *de poco a poco se anda lejos...* (Bit by bit we'll get there...)"

"Well, Sr. Teniente", said Megan, "you are welcome to stay in the guest room for as long as you like, look around, ask questions, but you will have to excuse us. Dying people don't wait for politicians to finish speaking,,!" and she got up and moved out.

Alberto finished his tea and continued some small talk, then Sheila Burns indicated the way towards the guest room and he asked her on the way over to the guest house how he might get into contact with the Spinks.

"Oh," replied Shiela in halting Spanish, "Well the Spinks work with the Mururuna Indians, that's some way away from here, but I know that my husband Mark is going down there to visit them sometime as they were at a School of Linguistics with us, so maybe we could fix it up for you to go. I'll talk to him about it tonight".

After a supper with the other people of rice and beans, Alberto spent the night in the guest room. It contained a wooden collapsible bed, a straw mattress, one sheet, a mosquito net, a small rickety table with a large tin basin, water jug, soap and a small towel. On one of the earthen walls there was a complex picture of two roads, one was wide with lots of people on it and one was narrow with just a few wayfarers. It looked as if the wide road ended at a cliff edge while the narrow road seemed to go on to the horizon where the sun was just rising. Alberto couldn't make out all the faded English on it. He did notice, however, the number of spiders and the odd lizard on the walls, as well as various plump cockroaches in one corner by the bed. But sleep was what he wanted most and sleep was what he got.

The next day, wandering round the Bible Institute buildings and the hospital, he spoke to an old man who appeared to be one of the groundsmen and asked him what he thought of things?

"Well, Señor, I was brought up in the orphanage they used to have here and they looked after me pretty well. Of course, some of the old missionary ladies, who are all gone now, were quite strict, but maybe we needed that sort of care. The new ones at the hospital and Bible Institute treat us more like friends, not like things. The older ones still call us "boys" or "girls" even although we're married and have families and one insists on speaking in English all the time to her colleagues when we are in the room and says things about us in English, as if we didn't know or guess!

"I must say they pay fair wages and have enrolled us in the government's new pension scheme, something that a lot of other businesses in the area haven't done.

"There are about 48 churches in the local area now. My uncle Vicente was one of the first converts in the area, all these years ago. He was a drunk and one day he was passing the small room where the two English *Señoritas* were singing and preaching and he fell in love with the one with brown eyes. So, he began to attend all their meetings and eventually he accepted Jesus Christ as his Saviour and Lord. His life was changed and he eventually became pastor of the first church in the town here.

"He's a very old man now, never married, doesn't get about much, but he has a dog that's named Ana, the name of the first missionary who came all these years ago!

"Forgive me, *Señor,* I have to go and check the well pump down the hill there. Be careful as you walk about, there are a good number of snakes about at this time of year, most of them are harmless, but the *naka-naka* (coral snake) is small but deadly, but it's easily spotted".

●●●●●●●●●●●●●●●●●●●●●●●

ALBERTO'S FOURTH ENCOUNTER

It was arranged that Alberto and Mark Burns should set off early the next day. After an early breakfast of *Nestum,* the Burns kids' favourite cereal, and a cup of strong sugary coffee, the pair set off in Mark's ex-army jeep down the highway to Puerto Atalaya, on the confluence of one of the main tributaries of the Amazon and the river Pumamayo.

Puerto Atalaya was a typical Amazonian town on the banks of the river. The houses by the river were on stilts and the shopping street was set further back on higher ground. Along the bank were a multitude of canoes, small river boats, some barges and a smart oil company launch. Mark and Alberto worked their way along the river front, past bales of cotton, bananas, logs, sacks of this and that, until they saw somebody waving at them in the distance.

"That'll be don Guillermo Flores Pashonasi, he's going to take us up the river. Harold will have sent him down for us.".

They dodged burly men loading sacks of rice on to a barge and eventually reached don Guillermo standing by a twenty foot aluminium launch with a 28HP Evinrude outboard on its stern. Don Guillermo wore a pith helmet! Alberto was surprised to see a local in that gear, but don Guillermo wore it as a kind of trophy and a recognition signal. Everybody on the river knew don Guillermo, with his gold teeth and flashing smile and seriously long thumbnail that he used for all sorts of things. A bit like 'Captain Hook', Alberto thought!

"*Hola, compañeros*", he called out, then energetically shaking their hands and squeezing the life out of them with a massive bear hug, while causing the boat to rock dangerously..

"We're going upriver now. If you've got a hat, wear it! And, if you have dark spectacles, wear them. The sun striking off the water can easily give you sunstroke!"

He paused to shout advice to a youth who was struggling to control a *'peke-peke'*, a thirty foot log canoe, with its *Briggs & Stratton* engine.

Mark and Alberto sat down in the centre of the launch and adjusted their feet among the spare fuel tanks, odd pieces of rope, paddles and poles, a plastic 5 gallon bottle of water, some beer bottles, a tarpaulin and various other bits and pieces, including six Calor gas cylinders.

Don Guillermo pumped the outboard's fuel line, tugged the starting cord vigorously, checked the dribble from its water-pump overflow, engaged the prop, backed out into the greasy river and gunned the motor. Alberto fell back over the seat as he wasn't expecting such a quick start. He scrambled back into a sitting position and felt the refreshing breeze on his face as the river bank went whizzing by. A flock of green parakeets protested at the invasion of their privacy. Soon they had left the town far behind as they headed downstream on the nine knot current.

"In half an hour we'll turn up the river Arenasi. Don't know why it was called the Arenasi. Perhaps because the river has a sandy bottom and sand bars. Not sure why these Indians are called the *Mururuna* either. It might mean the *'Muru people'*. It's not what they call themselves in their own language. They call themselves *Nuwami,* meaning roughly *'We are THE people'*. Some say the Jesuits in the XVI century came through here from Ecuador and infected the tribes with *'Muru-onqoy'*, the bubonic plague. Those that survived were then called the *Murus*, but, who knows?"

They were approaching the mouth of the Arenasi. It was hard to spot for it was a mere twenty metres across, compared to the two hundred metres or so of the main river.

"Sometimes it's hard to get in here because of a *palisada* (log jam). In the flood season the river brings down lots of logs and debris. One year they had to dynamite the *palisada* to clear it".he added.

"The *Mururuna* bring their rice crops down on balsa rafts and this is the place that they get mostly stuck. But it was quite clear when I came down yesterday."

They steered slowly in across the current and soon the entrance was quite clearly to be seen between two high mud promontories. Don Guillermo steered close to the left side.

"The logs jam up under the surface on the other side", he pointed out as they coasted in.

Then they began the slow journey up river as it wound here and there. Sometimes there would be large sand bars across the bend, Through the brush from time to time one could see ox-bow lakes. In fact the whole area would become on big lake in the wet season.

"If you want, you two could go ashore and walk the next bend. It'll take as long by launch to go round the circle as it does to walk across the corner!"

Alberto and Mark declined, thinking about the snakes and other creepy-crawlies on the jungle floor.

Suddenly, the motor roared and the launch slowed to a stop.

"Hit something with the prop and that's the shear-pin gone! Fling out the anchor or we'll drift back to town!"

Guillermo was laughing as he yanked up the motor to examine the prop. The anchor itself was just an old cast-iron bracket. It would only take a couple of minutes for Guillermo to knock out the broken pieces of the copper pin and replace it with a piece from the copper rod in his toolbox.

"I just buy a length of rod and cut it to size, as we are forever shearing pins in this river, there is so much debris in it, as well as these hidden sandbars!"

Mark was interested in the technique. He would need to know these tricks as a pilot/mechanic! Alberto was looking at a large yellow sort of patch on the muddy bank up river. What was it? As they set off and passed it, he realised it was hundreds of yellow butterflies sunning themselves, beside what looked like a couple of logs on the sandbar. The "logs" were actually *caimanes* (alligators)! He began to feel a little unsafe in this smallish boat and wondered too if the river was full of *pirañas* as well! His fears were heightened when the launch later ground to a halt in mid channel.

"We'll have to get out and push the boat over this sandbar. Just hold on to the side and keep a good grip, because the channel will deepen very quickly once we're over these sunken logs. You steer, Mark."

The water came up to Alberto's knees, as he began to heave the boat along, with Guillermo doing the same the other side. He kept wondering about *caimanes* and *pirañas*! Was that a log he was trampling down or was it a *caiman*?

Suddenly there was no footing and Alberto sank up to his chest. Had he not had a firm grip he would have gone under. He hauled himself, dripping wet, back into the boat.

"Should be all right now", said Guillermo cheerily, "until the next one!"

It turned out there were two "next ones" before, two hours later, they drew into a high muddy bank with steps cut into it.

Standing twenty feet above them were a young *gringo* couple and ten or so *Mururuna* people, some with babies slung in shawls, barefoot and in an assortment of shorts and multicoloured T-shirts including one affirming that the owner was from Oxford University!

Don Guillermo jumped for the bank with a line and tied the launch up to a stake.

"*Hola*, here we are! You got the radio message then?".

"No", said one of the group, "but we dreamt you were coming so we told don Haroldo".

Alberto tried to look dignified as he jumped for the bank and tried scrambling up the steep muddy steps. It didn't work and he slipped and slithered back down on his hands and knees. Don Guillermo caught him and saved him going in the river.

"Just take it slowly. Here, use this pole to help you, I'll bring up the bags".

When Alberto and Mark eventually got up, one of the *Mururuna* came forward with a towel and a bowl of water to wipe Alberto's hands and knees, while another came forward with a gourd bowl of thick white liquid.

"Go on", encouraged don Guillermo, "it's *masato* made from the *yuca* (manioc) plant and fermented by the grannies of the tribe spitting into it! You have to drink it, it would be a discourtesy not to accept their welcome!"

Alberto closed his eyes and took a fearful sip. Actually, it was cool and refreshing.

He then turned to the young New Zealand couple, Harold and Martha Spink.

"Sorry you didn't get the message as to who I am and why I'm here to visit you today.".

"No", they replied, "but come up to our place and we can talk about it in the shade".

Their "place" was a platform with open walls and a palm-thatch roof on stilts, in a group of similar constructions that formed the village.

After Alberto explained something of his mission, Martha began:

"We've not been here long, the other older missionary couple left last week as they were due furlough. They have been here for five years. It use to be a six-year term in our mission and the oldies think we are wimps because we want to go back to our homeland after only five!

"But, it does take time to get to know the language, the people and their culture. An old missionary once said that for the first few years you should *'keep your eyes open, your ears open and your mouth shut!'* And when you think about it, Jesus was thirty years on earth before He began his ministry!

"We are trying to learn the *Mururuna* language and are going to help eventually to begin translation of the Old Testament books. They have the New Testament now, but you can't really understand God's plan fully without both.

Please sit down on these rush mats", she gestured with her hand. "The mosquitoes don't come out much till dusk and we have mosquito nets for your bed space tonight. We made it up now so the mossies don't get in later when it's dark!

"But you folks must be hungry, so we've got some toasted plantains, and 'chicha morada' to drink and then there are plenty *pawpaw* and coconuts around, oranges, or mangoes, if you like."

Alberto wanted to know why a lovely young couple would want to come to this remote, "primitive place", when they could be living in a beautiful prosperous country like New Zealand.

"Well, I guess that's easy to answer in one way. When God calls you, you gotta go!", laughed Harold.

"Explain that a bit more to me". Alberto was puzzled.

"Well, we were both brought up in Christian homes, went to church on Sundays, played lots of sport, rugby, tennis, surfing and things, got married and thought about starting a family. We both had good jobs, I was a rugby player and sports coach; Martha was a school teacher, but somehow life didn't seem to have much meaning. One Sunday a man came and talked about mission work in South America.

He said one funny thing though, '*You don't become a missionary by getting on a plane*'. Then he went on to explain it was important for Christian folks to ask God, what was His '*good, acceptable and made-to-fit will*' for our lives. We'd never thought of asking God about that, so one afternoon we went down to the beach, sat on a rock, and said to God:

'*Okay, God, what to you want us to do? That's what we really want*'.

"Well, we didn't hear a big trumpet telling us! But we began to find out about opportunities and gradually three years later, after doing some further studies, we have landed up here! And it is so neat!"

Alberto thought he couldn't do "neat", but he admired their enthusiasm and wished that many in the Revolution would have shown that zeal, instead of being self-seeking *chupa medias* (sock-suckers) like himself.

In the afternoon, they wandered around and watched the children playing in the river; some men were preparing a raft from balsa logs and tying them together with 'vines' festooning the neighbouring trees; women balancing pots of water on their heads were coming up from washing clothes at the river's edge. Alberto spent some time trying to locate the different multi coloured birds and parrots that flitted through the forest.

One of the *Mururuna* pointed out the various types of trees on the opposite bank: *Canela Muena, Uchu Mullaca, Poloponte, Capirona, Mashonaste, Tangarana, Lupuna* and many others.

"They all have *almas* (souls), *Señor.* The *Tangarana* has a "*mother*", the biting red ants that live in it and look after it if anyone bumps into it or tries to cut it down. The *Lupuna* thinks itself very important with its big bulging trunk, but when you cut it down, it is all spongy inside and not even useful for firewood. *Sí, Señor,* the forest is alive and teaches us many things".

Around four o'clock Alberto and Mark were summoned for a meal. They sat in a circle round a piece of ground that appeared to be emitting steam.

"This is a *pachamanca*", explained Harold. "You dig a hole, heat a pile of stones on a fire, place them in the hole and put your meat and veges in, cover it up with banana leaves and mud and leave it to slow cook".

One of the tribe began to sing in a high pitched voice and the others joined in.

"They are thanking God for the meal; they killed a wild boar with their blow-pipes yesterday and the meat is roasting in there now. With a blow-pipe you have to get within about 10 metres of the animal, not like with a shotgun or rifle. But they can "call" animals to them by imitating them and that's something we've lost the art of doing. Pity", Harold admitted.

After the meal Harold suggested they all go for a wash, not in the muddy river, but in a clear stream and waterfall not too far away. Alberto had never seen such a beautiful place. It was in a little gorge, the waterfall was only about 4 metres high but fell like lace and one could get in behind it and sit alone and listen to its gentle fall. He began to realise there were bonuses for living here after all and he was surprised how cool the water was.

As it got dark the '*chicharras*' (crickets) began their chirping.

"Time for bed", Guillermo said and slapped his neck as the first of the mosquitoes moved in for their supper!

Their beds were woven mats from the '*poloponte*' bush and the mosquito nets hung above them from the thatched roof. Guillermo gave Alberto a little '*alcusa*', an old *Carnation Milk* tin filled with kerosene and a cotton twist wick, as a bedside light.

"Just leave it by your bedside lit in case you have to get up in the night".

The bedroom was just another open platform at the end of the house, so that as Alberto lay there and tried to find a place where his bones did not seem to stick through to the mat, he could see a myriad of stars through the trees. Eventually, though, he fell asleep. It had been a long day.

Early in the morning he was awoken by someone intoning something in the tribal language. Whoever it was went on and on and on. Eventually Alberto was forced to get up and was surprised that he was last on the scene. He moved through to where Martha was sitting cross-legged, plucking a dead hen.

"Who is that fellow out there going on and on about something?"

"Oh, that'll be Hildefonso, the tribal elder. He is reciting the New Testament in his language. He knows it all by heart! You see that's another thing we can't do any more, we have lost the power of oral memory! We are so used to reading and writing or recording things or listening to things, we have no long-term memory anymore. That's why, for example in the Old Testament, you have long genealogies because people were used to being able to remember all their ancestors. It seems a pity to me, sometimes, that we got "civilised!""

After breakfast of rice, beans and *plátanos* (boiled green plantains) Alberto and Guillermo said farewell to Martha and Harold, to Mark, who had decided to stay on for a day or two, and then to the *Mururuna.*

One of the *Mururuna* had asked who Alberto was and when Harold tried to explain he was from the government, the comment was:

"Government of what, how can they govern the river, the forest or the animals? Why, he didn't know any of the trees or animals in this country by name!"

As they drifted off down river Alberto thought, how was he going to get back home to the Capital? He was up a river in the middle of nowhere, on the wrong side of the Andes and he was supposed to report to Ernesto in four days' time. And what was he going to say?

While he sat peering again at the twist and turns of the river, Guillermo suddenly gave voice to his questioning.

"So, how are you going to get back to the Capital? Of course, there is a plane service from two days down the main river that would take you over to the coast, but it's been a bit hit and miss since the Revolution. But, look, I have a friend who has a Cessna 180 who flies from here to the highlands, up to *Cerro Blanco,* twice a week and from there you could get a bus down to the coast and on to the Capital. That would be just as cheap and more interesting than a regular flight on the State airline."

Alberto remembered that he had not yet interviewed this person, Joseph Richards, from Jamaica, and that he lived in a coastal town. Maybe he should make the effort to squeeze that visit in.

"Bueno, ¿dónde se encuentra tu pata (Well, where do I find your mate)?"

Guillermo looked a little sheepish.

"Look," he said, "his runs are not really "official", so can I count on you not to mention anything about them when you get down to the Capital or to any of your friends in the military?"

Alberto was getting a little tired of all this roughing it in this, his country, so he was willing to take his chance with this friendly offer.

"*Cuenta conmigo* (Count on me)", he replied.

"Okay," said Guillermo, "like the monkeys, '*see nothing, hear nothing, say nothing*'. I'll drop you at the *Hostal El Sol* at the port and I'll call for you when the flight's on."

They said very little in the next few hours as they made their way slowly back to Puerto Atalaya.

At six the next morning, there was a tapping on Alberto's door and a voice said "*Listo Calixto*" (Ready then).

Alberto hurriedly dressed, sloshed his face with water, grabbed his belongings and went down the stairs to find Guillermo waiting with a taxi. They went off round the back of the town and gradually became surrounded by bushes and scrub as the track became more rough and uneven. Half an hour later they eventually broke out into a three hundred metre clearing and at one end sat a *Cessna 180,* covered in camouflage netting.

Guillermo introduced the pilot as '*Paco*' but Alberto was unsure of his nationality. His Spanish was not the same as his and he noted that the plane didn't have his country's national registration marks.

Two men were loading boxes of fruit into the cabin and finally two black sacks that seemed quite heavy, knobbly and bulky. There were a few fuel drums of aviation fuel standing around, but the two loaders seemed unconcerned as they continued smoking, refuelling and loading at the same time.

Guillermo shook hands briefly with the two men and went off in the taxi. Alberto began to wonder if this was an illicit *narco* setup? Should he refuse the flight, attempt to call the military, or the police? But he knew no-one, or where the military base was and he also knew by the look of the .45 stuck in the pants of the pilot, that by the time he got his service revolver out of his bag, things would be beyond his control. He opted to do nothing, for who would know?

Paco motioned for him to step up into the cabin and sit on top of a box of oranges. The black bag felt uncomfortable against his back but he pulled on his safety harness and waited for the men to remove the netting while Paco checked the plane's flaps, rudder, kicked the tyres and pulled the prop over a couple of times. He too then climbed in.

Switching on the controls, Paco adjusted his mike and altimeter, and pushed a red button. The engine wheezed and coughed and then burst into life. He revved it up a couple of times, checked the gauges, waved briefly to the two men and began to taxi to the far end of the field before swinging round to the face the way they had come.

"Here we go!" he yelled.

He stood on the brakes, revved the engine up to full power, the plane shuddered and shook and then leapt forward over the grass. Alberto saw the trees coming closer and closer and, at what seemed the last second, Paco pulled the stick back and they skimmed over the tops of the forest and out over the river.

Alberto started to breathe again.

Soon they were gaining height, but the hills and mountains always seemed to be reaching up for them. Their altitude increased, two hundred metres, three, five, eight, one thousand, two, three thousand, and still the mountains were just outside the window. The plane bucked and bobbed in the updraughts, the black bag dug more deeply into Alberto's back.

"What's in the bags?"Alberto shouted to Paco.

"Dollars... ", replied Paco unconcernedly.

"Dollars!"

"Yep, probably about sixty thousand dollars in each sack in five and ten dollar notes. Payment for the shipment of cocaine paste that went out last night. I'm taking the dollars somewhere where they'll be picked up for "laundering"- probably turn into a fleet of cars or maybe that new airport building, who knows!"

"Do you do this often?"

"None of your business... but what else could I be doing down here to make money?"

Alberto decided to say no more.

They were flying down a long mountainous valley now and Alberto could see a road running alongside the river. There were only a few houses scattered here and there.

"Get ready to help me, I'm going in low in a moment over that village and when I say, loosen your harness, open the sliding door and chuck the two bags out! Ready!"

What was there to do? He was part now of a *narco* operation!

"Now!" yelled Paco.

Alberto squirmed round, slid back the door and with his foot booted the first bag out then grabbed the second and flung it out as well.

"Shut the door!" Paco banked away to the right. Had it not been for a grab handle, Alberto would have been a "package" as well, going to the valley floor!

"Suppose someone else picks them up, or they go in the river?"

"*No tiene nada!* (Makes no difference) What's one hundred and twenty thousand dollars in our business? Anyway, everybody is a winner, no?"

They landed twenty minutes later in Cerro Blanco's small airport, just long enough to unload the boxes of oranges and for Alberto to be glad that was all over.

He made his way to a military policeman who was standing guard at the office, as Paco flew off to the south.

"Did you see that plane that just landed? I think it's in the *narco* business. You should have arrested the pilot and detained the aircraft."

"What plane, sir?" asked the policeman, "No planes have landed today so far, just some aircraft noise from engine run-up testings."

Alberto gave up and walked out of the little airport, looking for the bus station.

He was glad to discover that an interprovincial bus was about to leave for the Capital in about an hour's time. He booked a ticket, asked if he could leave his bag in the office and went out to look for a café. It was now mid-day but still not too warm and not a cloud in the sky. He ordered coffee and a couple of bacon sandwiches and reflected on life for a moment.

His tour hadn't been that bad, he had met a lot of interesting people, had several "adventures", seen lots of new things and had begun to realise two things.

His country wasn't just the Capital, but a multi-faceted world and the Revolution would have to take that into account. Secondly, there seemed to be more to life than just "getting on" and maybe these missionary folks had found something, or was it somebody? - and that was something he didn't have. Maybe when he got back to the Capital he would do something about it, go into the cathedral across the road from the office and pray or something, he didn't exactly know what. Maybe he could talk to that Mary girl about it.

The bus was half empty when it eventually set off.

There were three *Sinchis* in the front seats, their sub-machine guns dangling in the netting above the seats. Alberto hoped the safety catches were on! The rest were locals going to the Capital, perhaps to migrate there, or to visit families or to do a little *negocio* (trading). When he was boarding he had seen the *choferes* (drivers) stuffing two live goats into a compartment at the rear of the bus, obviously to make a little money "on the side",

The bus climbed slowly out of the town, stopping at the *tranca* (highway control) at kilometre eight on the route to the Coast.. The military police boarded and asked for documentation and began to search the bus. The lady behind him was hauled off the bus - they had found a suspicious packet under her seat. It contained *pasta básica* cocaine. She squirmed and screamed that it was not her packet, and Alberto had a shrewd suspicion that someone else on the bus had shoved it there at the last moment on seeing the police coming onboard. But the bus was soon to continue on its journey leaving her screaming and protesting at the roadside control.

The road continued winding its way up the valley to the pass and beyond and into the late afternoon sunshine. Alberto dozed and dreamed of his flat and his friends waiting for him down in the Capital. He watched the distance markers go by. Kilometre 20, 30, kilometre 35 and there he saw a condor wheeling over the far side of the pass. They were starting down the other side in a series of tight curves

He didn't expect the sudden skidded stop as they went round the next blind curve. He banged his head on the head-rest in front of him.

There, through the windscreen, on the road in front of him, were two other coaches with smoke and flames billowing from them and a small crowd of people standing around in confusion! His driver swung on the lever of the door, darted out and leapt off down the mountainside.

As the *Sinchis* struggled to disentangle their weapons, the windscreen of the bus shattered and "zip-zip-zip" of bullets entered the bus. The *Sinchis* fell like wooden dolls in a heap as Alberto tried to cower down for protection. Then an armed masked man appeared in the door, with a battered felt set at comical angle and with a poncho over his shoulders.

"Apuráte, ¡qué bajen todos! (Quick, all off!)", waving his weapon wildly.

It was not easy to step over the bleeding corpses and get down. Some passengers exited through the emergency door and stood huddled together with Alberto and others at the roadside

"Any more police or military here?" asked the man with the funny hat.

Alberto went cold at the back of the group. What if they searched him and found his identity document? What if they found his pistol in his bag? With a sleight-of-hand movement, he got his wallet out of his hip pocket and tossed it in the deep drainage ditch behind them.

Some others of the terrorist group were going through the baggage on the roof of the bus.

They found Alberto's military revolver.

"Whose is this?" another terrorist asked from on top of the bus. Alberto struggled to think if anything else in the bag could identify him. He said nothing and others said little either, though two of the women were sobbing and a little boy was clinging like a limpet to his dad, face buried in his dad's poncho.

"Okay, you all have ten seconds to say, or we'll shoot you all."

Alberto looked at the child and said,

"It's mine, '*jefe*', a friend gave it me".

"Get over there", pointing to a place a couple of metres up the road.

Alberto slowly made his way over to the spot. This was going to be it. 'May God forgive me for all my ways', he thought.

Two other terrorists meanwhile demanded that all the passengers take off their shoes and outer clothing and place them in a pile on the road. The piles grew, the passengers shivered. The terrorists were either barefoot or had rubber-tyre sandals. One began to throw petrol over the bus's interior and the man on the roof, still pointing at Alberto jumped down on to the high bank.

Slowly, as in a dream, Alberto began to hear the beat of a helicopter coming low up the valley below towards them. It was a military gunship. The terrorists heard it also and began scooping the clothes up into *llijllas* (coloured woven cloths) and grabbing what else they could from the baggage that lay strewn about.

Alberto saw the terrorist from the banking raise his AK47 rifle, He "saw" the bullets coming, as he dived backward headlong into the deep drainage ditch behind him. The terrorist didn't fire again, convinced he had killed Alberto, but set off after the rest up the hill, clutching as much spoil as he could carry, as the gunship appeared from below.

Alberto slowly climbed out of the ditch, he was alive!

He waved in acknowledgement to the army helicopter gunship, as did the other passengers surrounding the smoking wrecks.

Then Alberto and the others saw and heard the gunship open fire!

•••••••••••••••••••••

ERNESTO'S SECOND ENCOUNTER

It was a "mistake"! The Group-Captain from the central division of the Helicopter Attack Squadron explained to Ernesto later that week:

'The commander of the aircraft thought that those by the buses were the terrorists and the ones running away were the passengers! They all look equally scruffy, armed and dangerous up there. I am deeply sorry about your colleague. Of course, he will get a posthumous gallantry medal and his family a pension".

"Lieutenant Alberto had no family, as far as I know", Ernesto said quietly, "but I'd like to have the medal here in the office, the staff liked him".

"It's quite a shock..." he added, standing staring over at the cathedral clock.

"You get used to it, where we are", grimaced the Group Captain. "We are killing our own countrymen or being killed by them almost daily at the moment. You don't know who to trust up there among those "*indios*" and "*charapitos*" (highlanders and jungle dwellers)

"Well, I must be going. Nice to meet you!".

The Group-Captain saluted with a flourish and went out, closing the door quietly behind him.

Ernesto stood silent for some time until the cathedral clock reminded him where he was.

"Maybe I should finish what Alberto started, though I've no idea what he made of all the visits he did, or even where he went", he thought.

He looked again at the list that he kept in the bottom drawer. The only names left were this Jamaican fellow and another couple up the coast. Well, he could ask for a week's compassionate leave and go up that way; the surfing beaches were nice at this time of year.

Pushing back his chair, he went out to the outer office to find a clerk to write his official leave request. One of them obviously had been crying. He assumed that the Group-Captain must have mentioned about Alberto on his way in or out.

"I'm sorry that you have heard about Capitán Alberto's sudden death", purposely bumping up Alberto's rank. "He must have been very gallant and done all that he was doing to further the Revolution's cause.

"Excuse me, what is your name?" addressing the tearful secretary.

"Flor de la Mancha Rojas", she replied, still sniffing slightly.

"Bueno, Flor, could you write me out a request for sick leave starting from Wednesday, and leave it in my in-tray to sign tomorrow, thanks".
Ernesto went on out and round for his car. The beggar was still there. This time, still thinking about Alberto, he left a couple of coins in the can.

"*Dius pagarsunchi* (May God repay you)", whined the beggar.

Wednesday turned out to be one of those days in the Capital where everything was grey and drizzly. It rarely rained properly and as bus and taxi drivers' vehicles suffered from stolen windscreen wipers, so traffic was slower and drivers more irritable than usual. Horns blared, lights flashed, hands banged on car doors and buses failed to stop for soggy people when they waved them down. So, Ernesto was glad to make it across the city to the airport, at last. He had given himself extra time.

It was just an hour's flight up the coast to Burgos, a city named after the one in Spain by the *conquistadors* when they settled in the area centuries before. Burgos had numerous colonial buildings and was surrounded by ruins of pre-Columban archaeological sites that the tourists loved.

It was to be the first time that Ernesto would fly in a new jet passenger plane. He could not believe the difference! This BAC 111, how quiet it was and sumptuous, compared to the DC3 and DC4 unpressurised propellor aircraft that were still on all the other routes. The air hostesses were smart too, in their new national airline's colours and insignia. This was Progress! He was really impressed the way the Revolution was going, by all accounts, at least from the Capital's perspective.

He was impressed by the "real" cutlery and meal aboard, though he did notice the people opposite squirrelling away the metal cutlery and asking for as many free drinks as possible in the time!

Arriving at Burgos airport, he procured a taxi and set off for the Tourist Hotel. He would need to ascertain exactly how to find the Possilthwaites (what a mouthful!) and their orphanage and this Jamaican fellow. He was sure that the receptionist at the Hotel could direct him to them. He would visit this Jamaican fellow first.

The Orphanage turned out to be some 60 kilometres north of the city, near a village in the foothills. Ernesto decided to hire a car for the journey. The hiring company was not too keen to let their vehicles go out on country roads, but, after a bit of haggling and "pulling rank", he obtained a fairly decent looking Toyota.

The journey next morning was a pleasant one to begin with, up the *Panamericana Norte* highway, stretching in a straight line through fields and plantations of vines and *algaroba* trees.

He stopped at a wayside café for coffee and noticed that the large fields behind him were withered and barren. The new sign beside the café showed that the land was now the property of the *La Cooperativa Nu. 79, San Jacinto de Colmes.*

He moved over to the adjacent table where an elderly man was also drinking coffee.

"Excuse me, good-morning, can you tell me why these fields over there are in such a state?"

The elderly man laughed.

"That's the Revolution for you! These fields belonged to the *Hacienda San Jacinto* before the Revolution and were very productive with maize, sugar-cane, beans, rice… Then it became a Cooperative, supposedly *"for the benefit of all"*! But the government sent in young graduates from the Agrarian University in the Capital, many of whom had never been on the land before. They spent the grant money on a truck and a pickup and then they decided to plant beans for a cash crop. The locals told them it was too late in the season to plant beans, but they went ahead and spent the rest of the money on seed and a new Russian tractor as well!

"So they went ahead and ploughed up all the sugar-cane and planted the beans. The beans came up OK, but the water irrigation system from the hill country, over the back there, dries up in June and the beans weren't far enough on. They shrivelled and died, as you see before you!"

Ernesto turned back to the man, who continued,

"Their Russian tractor has broken down and the next big Cooperative has "borrowed" its wheels as their own tractor tyres from Roumania were useless. No one told them that their tyres were also put on the wrong way round!

The man was warming to his task!

"Then these young engineers crashed the Cooperative pickup going to a fiesta and the Cooperative truck was stolen in the Capital with the first load of fruit that they took. So far, the "members", the workers, have never been paid and now nothing much is happening. *'Viva la Revolución,' no?*""

Ernesto was shocked, but he assumed this must just be a "one-off," a "mismanagement" crisis.

As he drove on up the road towards the next river valley and its Cooperative, he noticed what appeared to be a similar situation of "mismanagement" when he turned in at its entrance, down a lane beside the fields. This was supposed to be near where the Jamaican lived and so he would enquire there.

He noticed a narrow-gauge rail track running alongside, presumably used to transport the sugar-cane to the refinery. Both the track and the fields were deserted.

At the end of the lane stood what must have been the refinery, also semi-deserted. In contrast, the workers' small houses were a hive of activity and thirty or forty children were there in the midst of some game of sorts, their shouts and screams reaching him from a distance.

He saw a banner draped over the corner of a larger building:

'*Escuela Vacacional de la Biblia, Bienvenidos a Todos* (Bible Holiday Camp, all welcome)!'

Stepping out of the car, he asked a lady sitting separating a pile of rice from its husks,

"Where can I find Señor Joseph Richards, a Jamaican?"

The lady pointed with her chin at a tall, young, athletic person who was directing a volleyball match between two groups of wildly excited children.

Ernesto walked slowly over to the game and had to return the ball that had come his way from a fierce blocking movement from the far side of the court.

"Are you Joseph William Richards?" he asked the young man, who had turned to watch him approaching.

"Yes, that's me, how can I help you?", while he kept one eye on the game and the score.

"I need to speak to you for a moment on behalf of the *Ministry of Immigration*".

"Just a moment 'til I get someone to continue refereeing here, then I'll be with you". He motioned for a young girl to take over.
"Let's go over and sit in the shade by that building there. It's the church here", motioning towards the hut with the banner.

They sat down inside the door, and Ernesto was surprised to see all the straw mattresses on the floor, and the benches piled up to one side. Obviously it was not like the "churchy" sacred spaces he had visited. There were no statues, no smell of incense, no stand with holy water, nothing save a painted scroll on the far wall that said, *'Solo Cristo Salva'* (Only Christ Saves).

"What do you do here?" Ernesto enquired.

"Well, I'm here for a couple of weeks from the town to organise and lead this holiday club for the kids on the Cooperative. As you'll have seen, the place is at a standstill and life is very hard at the moment, always has been in fact. Most of the men have gone off to look for work down at the port or the fishing. The families are subsisting by running their little vegetable plots and keeping the odd goat and chickens. So, the churches in the town, I mean the Evangelical churches, have organised this holiday club for the kids and also help with the food to run it for these two weeks. I work under them and they pay my salary".

Ernesto was astounded. "You mean you are not supported by imperialist agencies from abroad then?"

"Well, I used to be part of a foreign mission, but I felt I should be on the level with the locals and when our mission withdrew from the country because of the military and terrorist activities, I felt that as a Christian I should carry on and not run away, as it were. If they are my 'brothers and sisters in Christ' here, then I should be with them on the same level playing field, as long as I am not perceived a stumbling block." Joseph shrugged and smiled.

"Don't you miss Jamaica, your family and young friends?" Ernesto asked.

"Sometimes, yes, I do! But, as a Christian, I have many new 'brothers and sisters' here too, who think like me and support me, as I try and support them. We all belong to that 'other country and Kingdom that has no end.'"

"Are you a Christian?" Joseph suddenly asked Ernesto.

Ernesto was taken aback at this very direct question and approach.

No one had ever talked to him about his beliefs. It made him uneasy. He knew that in some areas of the country, the culture was such that direct speech was a common occurrence. He remembered once being invited to be a 'padrino' (god-father) for a wedding. He hadn't wanted to be, so he politely demurred and said he would think about it. His companion from that area, on hearing later about the incident, laughed outright and said,

"¡Ay, compadre, has aceptado entonces (Sorry mate, but you have actually accepted)!. If you didn't want to do it, you should have said '*No!*', and no one would have been offended!"

Ernesto glanced at the dusty earthen floor and muttered, "Well, I think I'm a Christian because I go to mass from time to time and after all, the Constitution says this is a Christian country under God".

Joseph laughed and slapped his leg.

"No, no! Being a Christian is something that you have to believe and do, like it says on the wall there. You need to be saved from your sins and God's judgement to come! And you need to do something about it, tell God you are a sinner, and ask Him to come in and change your life.

"Would you like to do that now?"

Ernesto was getting more uncomfortable. Somewhere deep inside him there was a voice saying that, 'yes, yes', he needed that something, somebody. Things were not what they should be with him, nor in fact what they should be for the Revolution. This Joseph guy was doing a good job here even it were only in a limited sphere. He could hear the joy in the kids' voices outside and seen it in their faces and in those who were accompanying them.

Ernesto shrugged his shoulders...

"Maybe you're right", he admitted, "but..."

Joseph put his hand on Ernesto's arm. "Don't do 'but'...Today, is the day of salvation, tomorrow, who knows...?"

Ernesto got up slowly and ,thanking Joseph, turned towards the kids and the car. He needed time to think, time perhaps to act. It would be a massive commitment. What would folks say in Immigration, in the clubs, in the Officers' meetings?

"Well, thank you, Joseph, I appreciate what your doing here, an eye-opener, but I must get on..."

"I'll pray for you", Joseph said solemnly, shaking Ernesto's hand.

"There's an Evangelical Church on block Sixteen of *Avenida Unión* in the Capital, you'd be most welcome there. A lot of your kind of people go there. You'd like it.

"Sorry, must get back to the kids, *Chau*!"

Ernesto backed the car out of the yard and turned down the track. He didn't know what to think.

•••••••••••••••••••••••••••

ERNESTO'S FINAL ENCOUNTER

The Possilthwaites were the last on the combined list and lived further up the *Panamerican Highway*. So Ernesto set off up the road again, past mile after mile of sand dunes on his right and the sea on his left. He slowed once for a stretch to watch some fishermen on *totora* reed canoes, balancing on the big Pacific rollers.

He knew the place he was headed for was called *Casa Urubamba*, an odd name for a coastal site, but *gringos* had odd ideas about names, and it was somewhere close to a village called *Playa Dorada*, a well known surfing venue, popular with surfers from all over the world.

When he arrived at *Playa Dorada,* he asked a barman in one of the beach bars if anyone knew where *Casa Urubamba* was?

Ernesto thought the barman gave him a funny look, but perhaps it was his imagination.

"Why do you want to know?" asked the barman.

"Well, I like meeting foreigners, and I believe they are an English couple running the place". It was a half truth, of course.

"Okay, if you follow the road north for ten kilometres, just past the 623km. road marker stone, then turn right up the track between the two sand hills, their big house is about a kilometre in. Oh, and watch out for the dogs! I'll phone them and let them know you're coming. What's your name again?"

Ernesto thanked the barman, told him his name, but not his title, finished his beer and got back in the car.

It turned out that it wasn't too hard to find the entrance, but there was no evidence of a habitation up the track. It was getting late in the afternoon and he was glad that the sun was behind him now, for it would have been difficult to pick out the track with the sun in one's eyes.

"Funny place to have an orphanage", he thought, but maybe there weren't too many large houses for rent around in the village.

The first sign of the place was two large Alsatian dogs that came bounding and barking from behind some low scrub. Then the house appeared round a corner, set in a high, wired compound. It looked very quiet, almost deserted. The front door opened and a doberman appeared, together with a tall handsome man with greying hair and dark spectacles. He was waving.

Ernesto ran the car through the open compound gate and up to the door, wound the car window down a little, as the dogs were still bounding and barking around him, and greeted the man.

"Good afternoon", he said in a loud voice, "I am Colonel Ernesto Delgado from the Immigration Service. I would like to have a little informal chat with you and ask how you two are getting on."

David Possilthwaite spent a few moments calling off the dogs and locking them into a room inside the porch. He then turned and welcomed Ernesto into a small lounge near the front door. His wife, Margaret, joined him. She was a large, florid woman, who obviously had some mobility difficulties.

"How can I help you?" asked David, "may I offer you a glass of the local wine? White or 'Seco'? My wife and I, as you know, run a home for disturbed orphan children here, that's why they are not in this part of the building and we try and keep them as undisturbed as possible".

"That's very honourable of you, Señores. How long have you being doing this?"

"Well, we have only been here for a couple of years; we were doing it in another Latin American tourist area but we had to move. We were sorry to leave the children there, although we did bring a couple of the older ones here with us."

"How old are the children then and how many do you have here?" asked Ernesto, out of interest, while sipping his wine.

"Actually, we have fifteen at the moment from eight to sixteen, two boys and thirteen girls, quite a handful!" replied the Señora. Margaret. "We have two helpers, they have been with us for a long time and are from the highlands."

He noticed that Margaret Possilthwaite was perspiring profusely and wiping her forehead from time to time with a large coloured handkerchief, yet the room with its high ceiling and circulatory fan was quite cool. He assumed it was due to her somewhat corpulent condition.

"Could I see some of the children,?" Ernesto enquired politely.

"I'm afraid that won't be possible at the moment. It's their *siesta* time and ,as they are quite disturbed, we don't like breaking into their routine, you understand".

Ernesto thought that five-thirty was a bit late for a *siesta*, but it would be good for him to get going soon and get booked into somewhere in the beach village before dark.

"Well thank you for the drink, this was just an informal visit. Your visa renewals should be through in a day or two. Enjoy you stay in our country". He rose and shook hands briefly with the pair.

"Oh, please don't loose the dogs until I get in the car!", he joked.

David Possilthwaite showed no emotion.

As Ernesto adjusted his safety belt, he glanced up at one of the windows on the second floor and saw two girls' thin faces.

They were holding a piece of cardboard with the word '¡*Ayúdanos!*' (Help Us!) scrawled on it. Then they suddenly disappeared!

As he drove away, the dogs following him, he wondered about the Possilthwaites and the place. Something wasn't quite as it should be, so different from his encounter with Joseph and his work earlier in the day. What was it?

He focused on getting back down the highway in the dark and into a beach hotel. It was pretty obvious that the first hotel he passed on the way into the resort was basically a brothel, so he opted for the *Queens Hotel* in the centre of the Promenade.

As he sat later in the evening, reading the newspaper and sipping a cocktail, he overheard two foreigners talking and laughing about the '*facilities*' on offer here in the resort.

"And," added one, "if you fancy young ones, I know where we can get one or two!"

The penny dropped! Ernesto would make some calls in the morning.

After a couple of days relaxing at the beach it was time for Ernesto to return to the Capital. He had made the phone calls to the respective agencies about *Casa Urubamba,* and felt good about that.

He returned the car at the airport early on the following morning and moved through into the airport foyer with his bags. The receptionist at the counter informed him that the flight departure would be on time, but the return flight today would take a little longer as they would be using one of their older aircraft, a jet turbo-prop aircraft, a *Lockheed Electra.*

Noting that he was a Colonel, she changed his seat booking to a more comfortable seat in the front section of the aircraft, took his bags and, after weighing them, tied the labels to them and gave him a boarding pass, advising him to go down to the right to *Gate 2*.

Ernesto sat awaiting the arrival of the aircraft and his call to board. As he did so, he could not help overhearing a conversation between two middle-aged aircraft mechanics, in the seats behind him, airport officials of some sort. He caught the words:

"... No, the new engines are still in Customs, the company has no money to get them out!", said one.

The other said, "Well, how many hours have the ones in that plane done then?"

"No idea," said the first man, "but at the beginning of last week they were over the limit and that plane's been on the States run twice since then!".

"Ah, well, that's my Latin America for you! At least our pilots are mostly all sober these days! *Viva la Revolución*! Back to the hangar, then..." The two men moved off through a door marked 'Staff only'.

Shortly after, the call came over the loudspeaker.

"Passengers for Aereolineas Costa A Costa, Vuelo 505, destination La Capital, please board through Gate Number 2. Have your identity cards, passports and boarding passes ready".

Ernesto hung back, no need to rush, as his seat would be in the front section. It looked like a full complement of passengers. When the queue had reduced to a trickle, he got up, went through the gate and on to the tarmac. The ground crew were refuelling the plane and a mechanic had the inspection hatch open on one of the motors. The baggage handlers were throwing luggage into the hatchway in the tail area.

Ernesto found his seat *A4* quite easily and accepted a copy of the '*Washington Post*' from the day before. He settled down for the hour's flight down the coast…

A couple of local boys were playing '*cops and robbers*' in the midst of the archaeological ruins just south of Burgos. The sky and the sea around them were clear and blue.

The boys heard the roar of Ernesto's jet turbo-prop on take-off one mile to the north of them, so they climbed up on one of the mud walls to get a grandstand view of the *Electra* climbing into the sky.

What they really saw was a fiery comet hurtling towards them; what they felt was an explosive impact that threw them backwards into the hollow below.

There were no survivors from the front section.

It was a Saturday, July 29th.

Two days later, Flor the typist took Ernesto's name plaque off the desk, emptied the drawers and closed the shutters.

She paused for a moment and prayed…

The cathedral clock struck twelve.

Made in the USA
Middletown, DE
25 January 2020